The
Faces
of
Love

(A Historical Novel)

Utta Pacenza

ARCHWAY
PUBLISHING

Archway Publishing books may be ordered through booksellers or by contacting:

Archway Publishing
1663 Liberty Drive
Bloomington, IN 47403
www.archwaypublishing.com
1 (888) 242-5904

Because of the dynamic nature of the Internet, any web addresses or links contained in this book may have changed since publication and may no longer be valid. The views expressed in this work are solely those of the author and do not necessarily reflect the views of the publisher, and the publisher hereby disclaims any responsibility for them.

Any people depicted in stock imagery provided by Thinkstock are models, and such images are being used for illustrative purposes only.
Certain stock imagery © Thinkstock.

ISBN: 978-1-4808-4026-3 (sc)
ISBN: 978-1-4808-4027-0 (e)

Library of Congress Control Number: 2016920274

Print information available on the last page.

Archway Publishing rev. date: 6/13/2017

Contents

Cover design by Utta Pacenza

Acknowledgements

To John,

the love of my life...

Prologue

Love can be a beautiful thing, as the saying goes "It makes the world go 'round." But, like in human families, Love can also have some unpleasant members, to name a few: jealousy, mistrust, greed—and even hate for a once-loved person, which could, in its worst case, lead to murder. Love in its purest form is the unselfish love of a mother for a wished-for child. After my own travels through life, I still believe in "Love."

I am lucky to find it in rewarding relationships with my friends. One special friend is "Melanie."

Like so many times before, she had invited me to enjoy a leisurely stroll in her garden and to check out the progress of recently bought plants. We are both garden enthusiasts and often share little excursions to different plant farms.

It was still early in the morning. The birds were tweeting the news to the other members of the flock that Melanie had replenished the food supply in the two seed boxes.

A soft breeze swayed the tall willow trees just enough to keep the temperature at a comfortable level before the summer heat would set in later in the day. Melanie, in wise foresight, had provided two easy chairs in the shade so that we could enjoy the morning air while chatting.

My friend often hinted that her life hadn't always been easy, and I was fascinated when she told me that she had spent most of it on two different continents. I didn't want to pry into her past by asking questions, but she volunteered by saying that one day she would confide in me. She looked like she wanted to talk so would today perhaps be the day?! To my surprise and delight, she seemed in the mood to begin her story . . . .

Chapter I

A s you know, I was born in Austria in a lovely small town on the outskirts of Vienna and the Vienna woods. Its founding history goes back many centuries and therefore attracts visitors from all over the world.

But as a child I was unaware of living in a historically important place. I was fortunate that I was born into a family with caring and responsible parents. My father came from Old Austrian aristocracy, of which I wasn't even aware until much later in life. Anyway, even then did I feel being different from anybody else. After all, what meaning has a title that one had not done anything to deserve. I was the youngest and had two sisters and one brother. I was a sickly child, so I guess I was a bit spoiled. Fortunately, my father was a doctor who kept an eye on me medically. He was a man of integrity who demanded respect, and never seemed to show much warmth toward us children, although I'm sure he loved us despite not displaying it. I think he probably was too busy providing for a growing family. His own father was a general and treated him and his two brothers as if they were Army Recruits! In the old Monarchy days, young officers had to marry rich - or at least well-to-do ladies - so that taking care of any resulting children would not be a burden for the government.

I remember as a child, I always had to curtsy in front of my grandparents and keep quiet for the rest of any visits. My grandmother looked like a woman whose spirit had been broken. She always seemed depressed and sat in a wheelchair with a blanket over her knees. As for being depressed, no wonder with a domineering husband like my grandfather. I was always scared of him, with his piercing eyes and a big mustache.

Later in life I was told that he had invested his wife's fortune into war bonds, and all this money was lost when the First World War ended in 1918. I'm sure that must have been devastating for my grandmother. I recall that my father often visited her and also took care of her as a doctor. Maybe she was the only source of love he knew in his own childhood.

Chapter II

D ue to the military tradition in my grandfather's family, it was obvious that one of the three sons should also become an officer. According to the "general," my father seemed to be the most suitable one. But Papa also wanted to become a doctor. It must have been an exhausting task training to become an officer, and at the same time studying to become a medical doctor. Perhaps his Army salary paid for attending the University. I'm sure he did not get much, if any, help from home due to the financial difficulties after losing the money from the War Bonds. Papa's struggles and eventual achievements probably made him the man he was, and therefore he expected us children to also accept our responsibilities and persevere in everything life demanded. Papa met my mother through one of her sisters who was his patient. My mother had just come out of her divorce and she had two young children from this marriage, a son Friedrich whom we later called Fritz, and a daughter called Carla. My mother told me much later in life that her former husband was a drunkard and gambler. Once she came home and all the furniture was gone. He lost it playing cards! Also there were constant threats from people he owed money.

In Austria we call our mothers Mama, Mami or Mutti. My Mutti was a beautiful woman and father fell in love with her and accepted her young family as if it were his own. Their first years must have been a struggle. I'm sure there was no help coming from grandfather, especially since Papa had married a divorced woman! They lived in a very small apartment on top of a butcher's shop. Fortunately, Papa had a contract as an officer and doctor in the Army. He could not open a practice as a doctor due to the lack of room. My sister Sigrid was born there and after a few years, I was on the way. Something had to be done! They had saved up enough money for a down payment on a house, so things started to look up. The house was really a big villa in a wonderful location with a huge garden like a park. The mortgage payments must have been huge, no wonder Mutti always had to keep our wishes down to earth. I remember whenever - as a teenager - I wanted something in the way of fashionable clothes or shoes (because some of my richer colleagues in school had it), Mutti always said "ask Papa!" And that took a lot of courage! Papa was not mean, but as a child you don't understand financial struggles of your parents.

About my childhood days I vaguely remember having been sick a lot, caught colds easily, and thus missed school frequently. Mutti's sister, Aunt Louise, was my godmother and a very loving lady. She was also a retired school teacher and she tutored me whenever I had missed school. With her help, I never even failed one grade. Carla had graduated from high school and trained for a secretarial position in a big firm. Sigrid showed musical talent, quit high school in the 5th grade, and enrolled in the musical Academy of Vienna to become a pianist.

Fritz was a doting brother to me. I adored him. He was the most talented one of all of us and always tried to give his best. He and another young man in his class – the later Austrian President Kurt Waldheim - both graduated from high school at the top of their class. Fritz was also a good athlete. Because he wanted to relieve Papa financially, he decided on a military career and joined 300 other applicants in the Austrian equivalent to "West Point" in the U.S., to become an officer. The applicants had to meet a very high standard, so out of the 300 only 8 qualified. Our Fritz was one of them. I missed him terribly, but whenever he was on leave, he let me wear his cadet's cap and "Bayonet," which was like a short saber on a belt. Naturally, I was glowing with pride, but all too soon he was gone again!

Chapter III

The years before the "Umbruch" - meaning something like a "turnover" - were very insecure and unrestful, with the stock market being in trouble and lots of people out of work. I was only 7 years old at the time, but I think Austria had then already been made into a Republic. There was a lot of talk about a guy called "Hitler" who was stirring the people with his promise to provide work and uniting Germany and Austria into one country or "Reich", which means "Empire." He blamed the capitalists, mainly the Jews, for causing the misery of the people. Papa had many Jewish friends who were fine people: doctors, scientists, musicians and painters. Papa was appalled and worried about the developments. But those public meetings with Hitler and his comrades spread like a disease and gained momentum. I remember one night when there was a lot going on in the streets, Papa closed all the shutters on the windows. We all gathered in a room with just a candle and were told to keep quiet. Fortunately, we lived on a small side street, so the mob concentrated their destroying activities in the town itself. As always, there are people who are envious of persons more prosperous than themselves. They won't hesitate to point their finger at them to get them into trouble.

I know they arrested the head of the local hospital, who was a friend of Papa, but unfortunately also a Jew. They put him into a concentration camp where these innocent and unfortunate victims were tortured and gassed. This was later called "the Holocaust," truly one of the darkest chapters in human history. Many years later this friend of Papa, who had miraculously survived, was rescued by the Americans from the concentration camp Theresienstadt after Germany had lost the war in 1945. When he returned to our town, he was a fatally ill and broken man. Papa, who was his doctor, then arranged for me to read for him twice a week because he was nearly blind.

Anyway, Hitler and his comrades won and Austria was renamed "Ostmark," which means something like a Bastion for the defense against the East, and we became part of the "Third Reich." Reich means Empire and Hitler declared himself "Reichskanzler" (Chancellor of the Empire). Soon after, the newly founded SA with brown uniform jackets and SS in black uniforms took over. They were called the storm troopers. They were the ones that acted the most brutal when arresting people. You could see them swarming all over the place. Freedom of speech was a thing of the past if you didn't want to finish up in a concentration camp. One had to be careful not to say a wrong word against the new system. Some people were quick to report you as being opposed to the new circumstances for their own personal advantages. If you happened to become a victim of such a report, you were quickly arrested and could say goodbye to your property, finances and freedom. Is it the three wise monkeys that advised: "see nothing, hear nothing, speak nothing?" It was a good example to follow in these days!

Chapter IV

T he only good coming out of the "new Germany" was that people were provided with work by building highways, and also because existing industries were converted to make weapons and other things useful for the "third Reich." Being only a kid, I did not understand the severity of the time and accepted circumstances as they were. We kids soon became organized into small groups with a "leader." We belonged to the "Jungmaedl" (young girls), proudly had to wear fancy uniforms consisting of black skirt, white shirt, white below knee socks with black shoes, a short uniform-type jacket made of sueded sand-colored fabric, and a small black triangle scarf held together by a plaited leather knot. I guess we thought we looked pretty sharp! I'm sure Papa thought differently! We had weekly organized meetings with acting out fairy tales and being taught how to create useful handmade items. Of course, politics turned into brainwashing and was not neglected. I actually enjoyed these meetings because I loved acting and creating and was good at it. As I got a bit older there was talk that I too could become a leader. When I proudly announced it to Papa he was horrified and wrote me a note to hand to my present leader that, due to my frequent sicknesses, I could not be relied upon. It worked! My possible "leadership" was never brought up again. I'm sure there was a sigh of relief from Papa!

Chapter V

When I think how we kids were taught to greet somebody in these days must have been almost comical. We had to throw up our right arm with outstretched hands and yell "Heil Hitler," meaning "Hail Hitler." Hitler appeared frequently in public with his SS storm-troopers or his SA as security guards and made speeches from a platform to masses of people. I can still hear his screaming loud voice, drumming his ideas of a "purified" Germany into people's heads. I remember all our birth certificates were scrutinized in case we had any Jewish blood. Later on, when we were already at war, we also had to shout "Sieg Heil" - hail victory - in those Hitler appearances. Papa had drilled us not to show any antagonism toward the new world we were living in. But, of course, at home we knew how Papa felt about the system. Recently, a friend from Austria sent me an old newspaper clipping from one of these Hitler speeches in our town. It shows a little girl standing in the foreground with crossed arms and a somewhat cynical expression on her face. That little girl was quite recognizably ME.

Fortunately Papa never saw it in these days; he would have given me a good talking-to about how, by my mocking expression, I could have endangered the whole family. Fortunately, if other not well meaning people saw it, they probably thought that I didn't understand what the speech was all about. The trendy "new look" in this new Germany Hitler must have adopted right from the Richard Wagner operas he adored. It was a young "Siegfried" look for the boys with blond hair and blue eyes. Even for the girls to be blond and blue-eyed was definitely an advantage. My brown hair and eyes were not part of the new German ideal.

I have always been a bit hazy to pinpoint the time of historical events, but I think Hitler was anxious to enlarge his empire, so he invaded Poland. It must have been not very long after he came into power. Italy feared the same fate as Poland so, under her leader, the Duce she became Hitler's ally. I remember both Hitler and the Duce appearing in the newsreel in Kinos (movie theaters) arm in arm, raving on to take over the world. I think Hitler's aggressive plans had France on his list as well. I don't remember exactly what brought it to a point, but I think the rest of the world wanted to put a stop to it. And all of a sudden, we were at war. Our villa had been classified as having more living space than was ruled, so at first we had to take in a young man from the SA and one from the SS. They were handsome young German men, and I think both Carla and Sigrid flirted with them a bit. It's the old allure of uniforms that make men so attractive to women! But soon they had to return to their outfits to "defend Germany."

We now had to move out of the upstairs rooms, because a German family with two young sons were allocated to take possession of it. I already saw two playmates in the sons and thought "hurrah," because nobody seemed to have much time for me in these days. Papa, however, soon stopped me from getting too friendly with them.

Anyway, true to Hitler's wishes, this family produced a new baby every year and the wife's sister arrived from Germany to help with the kids. I think the husband was provided with a high post in the Austrian mail system, a job that he probably took away from an Austrian. They were terrible boarders with all the kids running on roller skates and other vehicles on wheels across all the rooms upstairs. Sometimes we were afraid that our chandeliers would crash down on us.

We soon came face to face with what war was all about. Food supplies were rationed and allied planes started with the bombing. We were trained in what we had to do in case of a bomb attack, and in due course, industrial centers in Germany and Vienna and in the vicinity suffered big losses. Our small town was relatively safe as we had no industrial sites, but an anti-air raid tower close-by in the Vienna woods on a hill was the target of fierce activity. The anti-air raid guns were called the Flak. I think it means something like "the guns that protect from planes. "We had a warning system on the radio station. Whenever there was a threat of approaching bomber planes still far away, the radio station transmitted a sound like a cuckoo bird in intervals of a few seconds--we actually referred to it as "the cuckoo." Of course, all other radio programs were stopped. When the planes were approaching closer, a siren was sounded that we called " Flieger Alarm," meaning plane alarm.

When the alarm sounded, we were supposed to rush to the nearest air-raid shelter, usually a deep cellar in some public building or church. I was a nosey kid, stood under our big chestnut tree and was fascinated by the American planes slowly flying above in droves to deliver their deadly cargo on Vienna. I wasn't a bit afraid and stood there watching until worried Mama dragged me away to the shelter. The only bombs in our town were the ones that were left over from bombing Vienna and they wanted to get rid of before their return to the U.S. In my child-like fantasies, I wondered if the people flying these planes looked like the little men from outer space!

Chapter VI

P apa had worked terribly hard in these days. We rarely saw him. Being a Major and doctor in the Army, he had to go at 5 am to the nearby "Kaserne" where a lot of soldiers were stationed before they were sent to war. He had to examine the ones that claimed to be sick and attend to their medical needs. At 10 am he had to see patients at his practice in our house and, after a quick lunch, he had to make house visits to anybody sick. At 4:00 pm he opened his practice again to see more patients. He had no secretary; therefore, he also had to attend to all the paperwork and records himself. No wonder he was always grouchy with anybody sick in his own family. When I needed his medical attention, I once thought up a scheme. To the amusement of the other patients, I was hiding in a dark corner in the waiting room. When Papa opened the door and said "next please," my turn had come, so I marched into the examination room. He still looked a bit grouchy and growled: "What's the matter with you now!?" I think deep down he must have chuckled. With this heavy workload, it was inevitable that he suffered his first heart attack. Mami was terribly worried, and nobody could have done more to nurse Papa back to health. I remember that Grand-Papa, the "General," saw fit to pay us a visit while Papa was still recovering. He took Mami aside in another room and, as a kid, I could only assume that he told her off about something. Mami burst into tears and cried bitterly. Grand-Papa never really liked Mami. (I think the feeling was mutual!) He would have preferred Papa to marry an aristocratic lady and, of course, Mami was also divorced! Although I was always scared of the "General" I couldn't bear to see my Mami cry because of him, so I took him by the hand and led him to the door. He must have been so stunned that he actually did leave. I guess afterward, my knees must have buckled! Life had become very difficult and happiness seemed to have taken a leave of absence. With the frequent bombings, we often worried about Sigrid and Carla returning home from Vienna. Transportation sometimes was affected by the bombing and they had to walk home, which was a long journey. Fritz had been promoted to Lieutenant and came for his last short leave before he had to take charge of a company to lead into war against France. I remember it clearly. I was impressed by his new uniform and the big beautiful motorcycle he rode. Naturally, I followed him around like his shadow, but before he left, he wanted to be alone. From a distance I observed him walking slowly in the garden, sometimes stopping as if he tried to engrave it in his memory. I felt disturbed and could not help feeling that he was saying goodbye to everything he loved. I can still hear the roar of his motorcycle when he took off.

Chapter VII

After Fritz had left, I felt very sad and lonely. But I consoled myself that he would soon return like so many times before. Perhaps next time he might even take me for a ride on his motorbike?? I missed him terribly and whenever I passed his cello in the corner of his room, I always stroked it and tried to imagine the happy times before Hitler. We were a musical family and Papa often invited friends, who also played an instrument, for a musical Soirée. Papa himself played the piano, how good he was I couldn't judge as a tot, but naturally thought that he was wonderful. To stay out of the way of the grown-ups, I crawled under the piano when Papa played. Fritz made his cello "sing." Carla tried her best on the violin, and Mama was in charge to provide refreshments for the "musicians." Sigrid was still too young to take part musically, although she already took piano lessons. With all this music around, it wasn't long before I --at age 5--started tinkering with the piano keys, so it was decided I also should receive lessons by the same teacher. Those happy times of my childhood are unforgettable.

After Fritz's last visit, the house was very quiet and I was glad to have my girlfriend Petra living at the end of our small street. Our huge garden provided plenty of inspiration for all kinds of activities. There was also a very well built garden house that we made our headquarters. It even had an attic where hay was stored to feed our rabbits in winter. The balcony was our lookout from where we could spy on any grownups, especially Carla's and Sigrid's visiting boyfriends!! The war and its effects, even the occasional air-raid alarms, did not really concern us, and we didn't understand it anyway. Petra also had a brother who had to serve in the Army, and she missed him as much as I missed Fritz.

However, even we suspected that Hitler's war did not seem to go very well. Papa became more and more concerned. Hitler was losing control fighting on so many fronts at the same time. He even made the same mistake like Napoleon, when he sent ill-equipped troops into Russia in winter. The loss of lives was catastrophic. But the news the media projected were full of imaginary "victory bells." Papa secretly had started to listen to the English news in the cellar on a small short wave detector radio, so he knew the real state of the war. But by doing so, he endangered his and our lives had it been discovered. Hitler, including his closest equally crazy maniacs, still kidded themselves about the "End Sieg," meaning the "final victory. "I think a few of the very high ranking officers also realized the situation. To stop all the cruel loss of lives to continue, they planned to assassinate Hitler which went terribly wrong. Stauffenberg was one of these brave officers. He and some of the others were ordered to meet with Hitler and his still loyal commanders for a round table conference. The plan was to plant a satchel with a bomb next to Hitler, but by mistake it was kicked away from Hitler and the explosion only injured him slightly. Naturally the plot-planners had to face devastating consequences; they were abused and tortured in the most horrible way and suffered a terrible death when they were strung up with piano wires on butcher's meat hooks. I shudder to think what fate their families had to suffer. When Papa heard the news, he was emotionally distraught. He knew that we all would have to endure our fate to the bitter end.

Chapter VIII

When I look back what life was like in these days, I'm convinced that Mama had performed a huge labor of love--especially in winter. Yes, we did have electricity, but that provided no heating. Neither did we have gas for that purpose. That meant getting up before daybreak to stoke fires in the little stoves we had in some of our rooms. In the kitchen, the stove was also lit to cook breakfast and provide warm water to wash ourselves in small wash basins. I guess people of today find it hard to imagine what life was like without washing machines, dryers, refrigerators - not to forget "existing without cell phones." Papa had a phone installed in the house, but that was mainly for his use as a doctor so patients could reach him. The lack of a refrigerator was the least of our problems. Our house was very well built with thick walls and a cellar (basement) equal to the wine cellars that house the big barrels in the vineyards. Anything that had to be kept cool was put on the cellar steps. In winter, the space between the outside and inside windows did a similar satisfactory job. To stop the draft, we even had special pillows for that space to preserve the precious warmth in the rooms.

Laundry days meant extra hardship for Mami, but she never complained. Of course, whichever of us was available tried to help. But usually and sadly Mami was a "one woman band." In the laundry the clothes were boiled in sudsy water in a huge copper bowl with a wooden lid; it sat on top of a fire and was enclosed in a concrete cubicle. Papa had extended it to the next wall to form a ceramic tiled bathtub, so this copper bowl performed double duty by heating our bathwater as well. But back to the laundry. After the clothes were boiled, they had to be heaved out with a wooden stick into the tub for rinsing and then the water had to be rung out with "muscle power," put into buckets and had to be carried down into the garden to hang on the washing lines. We had a lot of trees, so the lines were strung around the crowns from tree to tree. Because the washing was still very heavy with water that couldn't be rung out (no spin-dry like in today's washing machines!!!), we had to support the lines with special long sticks that had a "V" cut out on top, so the lines could sit in the V, and this way our washing didn't drag on the ground. I will say that when dry, the clothes had a lovely smell and sleeping on such bedding produced the most beautiful dreams!

In winter, Mami's task was not any easier, because it meant carrying the washing up three flights of stairs into the attic. In freezing weather, we were warned not to accidentally brush against any of the garments, because being frozen stiff, a sleeve would just break off! Mami's wash-day ordeals remind one almost of the hardships the first settlers had to face in the west!!

Chapter IX

Mama had taken it upon herself to put food on our table. Everything was rationed and certain things were either unobtainable or the rations were next to nothing. She started a vegetable garden, planted corn and canned the harvest from our fruit trees for winter. She also raised rabbits, but I thought that was to provide me with playmates!! It never dawned on me that the occasional lovingly prepared breaded cutlet on our plates had anything to do with the disappearance of one of my "friends." When I asked, I was always told: "It had run away." One of my favorites had grown into a beautiful big male, and I could carry him on his back like a baby. He was allowed to run in the garden under my supervision and came when I whistled so I could pick him up.

It was a day like any other when lunchtime came, and I was hungry. I thought I had still time to quickly go and visit my pet before I would be called to the table. But his cage was empty so I thought somebody may have let him out in the garden, and I was going to look for him straight after lunch. Looking down on my plate, I saw the now familiar piece of breaded cutlet. Hungry as I was I took one bite but I couldn't swallow it. The horrible truth hit me why my pet's cage had been empty. I was violently sick and ran from the table crying hysterically. I went into hiding and could not be consoled "that he was in Heaven." I thought "How could he be in Heaven when he was on the plate?!"

Mama, who had not been aware of my deep attachment to my pet, apologized to me much later in life. She said she had never forgiven herself for the hurt she had caused me. Of course, I forgave her. She only tried to feed us the best way she could in these hard times.

However, I could never eat a furry or feathered animal that I knew, nor could I ever boil a live lobster! With my love for animals I really think I should be a vegetarian!!

Chapter X

It was the summer of 1942; both Petra and I were happy that we could enjoy our vacation without school. As usual, Petra had promised to come in the afternoon so that we could play in the garden and plan our activities for the next day. While waiting for her, I was hanging around in the front yard watching the goldfish in the fountain, when I suddenly saw Papa standing at a window in his surgery. He was reading a piece of paper, and his face looked pale and frozen. But then Petra arrived and I forgot all about it. Late afternoon, when I came in from the garden, there was a deadly silence in the house! Mami was nowhere to be seen and Carla, although home from Vienna, had disappeared too. There was an unusual quiet in the house that disturbed me and that I could not explain.

Papa had finished the afternoon session with patients, so to break this worrying situation I ran to him with a happy face. But he took me by the hand and made me sit on his knee, which was most unusual for him. Then he broke the news to me that Fritz had fallen in a fierce battle in France. I could not imagine that it meant I was never ever going to see my beloved brother again! How Papa broke the devastating news to Mama, I can hardly imagine!

Mami never got over it. Before that, she had been a happy fun-loving woman with a wonderful sense of humor. She lost a lot of weight, and she and Carla wore black for quite a while, as was the custom in these days. I was terribly sad, but my young age carried me over the shock a little easier. Of course I missed Fritz, but I carried all the happy times with him in my heart. In all my romantic encounters later in life, I always looked for this unconditional protective love in a man like Fritz had given me, but I only found it once very late in life.

Chapter XI

Despite everything that had happened, we all tried to cope the best we could. But even I, in my childish outlook on life, realized that nothing was ever going to be the same again. Mama put on a brave face, but it was sad to see the change in her. Papa was as busy as ever and looked very tired. Carla was still working for the same company in Vienna. When she came home, she spent her time with Mama, probably comforting one another over the loss of Fritz.

The news about the war still consisted of fantasies about the "victory," but many people started to have their doubts, which could only be expressed to trustworthy friends. Sigrid was practicing the piano very hard and even took part in concerts in Vienna's most beautiful concert halls that were arranged by the Academy of Music where Sigrid studied. I was taking ballet lessons at the time and fancied myself as an up-and-coming prima ballerina. I was dancing around the piano when Sigrid practiced and that drove her crazy and probably interrupted her concentration. Sigrid and I did not get along very well, so we had many verbal fights. She could be very nice, but even Carla and I agreed that she had inherited a lot of grand-papa's genes, and among ourselves we even called her "the General."

However, deep down I loved Sigrid as my sister, and because I knew all the difficult passages in the music whenever she had to play in a concert, I was in agony in case something went wrong. I had a little silver clutch bag that I pressed so hard that all the silver was on my hands with nothing left on the bag! So much for sisterly love!! Fortunately, any air-raids took place during the day so we usually had no interruptions in any of the concerts at night. Many of the young artists later became very well known, some like Friedrich Gulda even internationally. For me it was a wonderful experience and probably an important factor for my love of classical music. I think Sigrid was 18 or 19 years old and had fallen in love with a talented young flutist she had met at the Academy. He had just passed his final exams and had accepted a post as a flutist in the Philharmonic orchestra in Frankfurt, Germany. Unfortunately, Frankfurt was being heavily bombed at the time, which was very worrying. Therefore, Sigrid was euphoric every time a letter arrived to prove that he, Nicholas, was alright.

Nicholas' father was French, a radio lecturer who must have married a very rich lady, because they lived in a beautiful villa on top of a hill in the Vienna woods, overlooking Vienna. The surrounding vineyards also belonged to them. Papa had met both Nicholas and his father (whom we called "the professor") and was impressed by both.

Today I'm surprised that they--being French--apparently had no problems with the Nazis, because we really were at war with France!! Perhaps they had dual citizenship and had renounced the French??

Well, anyway, lucky for Sigrid there didn't seem to be a problem. I liked Nicholas right from the start and we became good "buddies" later in life.

Chapter XII

I must have been 11 or 12 years old. It was the middle of winter; we have had some snow and Petra and I wanted to go see a movie. Being the weekend, there was an early show in the afternoon. Mama already had hot water from the copper filled into the tub so that I could have my bath before my date with Petra. It was lovely to soak a bit, the water just being the right temperature. The laundry room was nice and warm and made me feel as if I wanted to stay forever. All of a sudden I remembered my date with Petra, and I knew I had to hurry. So, with one leg still in the tub, and trying to dry the other leg on top of the adjoining stove, I slipped on the tiled tub floor and that pushed aside the wooden lid that covered the copper bowl with the boiling water. I fell into it with my left foot and right arm. I had such a shock, I turned on the cold water tap and held my injuries under it. The pain was incredible!

The laundry was not yet connected to the house, and stark naked as I was, I ran through the snow into the house screaming hysterically. Poor Papa, who had just gone down the cellar for a supply of coal, thought that somebody had tried to murder me. But, being the doctor he was, he calmly took me into his surgery and virtually "peeled" off the worst skin parts. Fortunately, being a weekend, he was home. The next weeks were awful.

I don't remember the exact treatment, but when new skin eventually formed, there was no scarring and now--in my older age--this horrible accident remains only a memory. It certainly was my good fortune that "there was a doctor in the house!" Carla was visited by a nice young man who was a soldier on a short furlough. I was still laid up in bed with a lot of pain. The arm seemed to be the worst. Although bandaged, I could only stand the pain if I was holding it upright. Carla's boyfriend was very sympathetic and promised, when he came home next time and my injuries were healed, he would take me for a sleigh ride. I thought that was very nice. By the way, his name was Fred.

Chapter XIII

The propaganda war-machine went on relentlessly despite all the bombings and destruction. Petra's brother had been reported missing in action fighting in Russia, but at least hope remained that he might return once the war would come to an end. "When will it end, or will it ever end?", everybody seemed to ask. Hitler and his faithful "madmen" still dished out in the news that the German "Reich" (Empire) was invincible. They must have been the only ones to believe it. But the allies in the rest of the world had already planned their final strategy to end the madness. It began on June 6, 1944, with the invasion of Normandy. A cleverly planned coup that must have been hell for the invaders brought out all the heroism and bravery men are capable of.

As for Hitler, he had spent the evening before with his propaganda minister, Goebbels, sitting around a pleasant chimney fire in his headquarters on top of the Obersalzberg in Berchtesgaden. Naturally, they would have been fantasizing about their final victory, and he never went to bed until 3 a.m., so nobody dared to wake the "Fuehrer" (leader) before 10 in the morning to tell him about the Normandy invasion. Therefore, the two tank battalions that were kept on standby around Paris were not alerted in time. When Hitler finally gave the order for them to attack, it was already too late. One could say: It was the beginning of the end. It was interesting to see that even some of the true Nazis seemed to realize it.

Besides Papa there were four or five other doctors in our town. I know that it is a doctor's code of honor to never say anything bad about a colleague, but within our family we surmised that Papa was not impressed by them. Strangely enough, all of a sudden Papa was the only doctor left in town. Even the Postmaster and his family upstairs packed up ready to leave in a hurry, with the explanation "that he had been appointed to another important position in the "West," meaning Bavaria and Salzburg, from where the Americans were approaching.

The war certainly came closer, with the Russians heading toward us from the East. Whoever of the Nazis feared for their future, naturally preferred to be under the Americans and departed if they could.

Papa decided we would stay; not only did we have nowhere to go, but Papa found it was his duty to remain, being the only doctor left in town. There were no able-bodied men left, only 14- year- old boys, old men, women and children. However one still had to be careful not to say something negative that could arouse suspicion because the remaining "officials" would not hesitate to take the law into their hands and order executions.

Papa received orders that he-as an officer-was to lead a group in The "Volkssturm" (folk's storm) to resist the approaching enemy. This group only consisted of some 14- year- old boys and old men. You could compare it to the last flickering of a flame ready to go out. Papa told us to lock ourselves in while he was gone. From faraway we could already hear gunfire. We were scared and worried sick over Papa's safety.

Chapter XIV

When I woke up next morning like a miracle Papa was home again! What a relief that was! We could hear gunfire much closer now; it seemed almost as if it was right in our town. Papa said, having been in command of the little group of young boys and old men, he could not see any sense in resisting the approaching "enemy," so he sent everybody home to be with their families. I was still kind of drowsy and, with our "protector" being home, almost fell asleep again. But just as I was dozing off, there was a loud banging on the door. My bed was in--what we called the "garden room"--because the door opened to a little terrace that led right into the garden. Papa rushed to open the door - two Russian soldiers pushed past him. One was a short Mongolian, moving swiftly like a weasel, and Papa had trouble following him right up to the now empty first floor, which left me with the other one -- a tall blond guy with quite a nice face and reasonably clean looking. I was scared stiff, but when he saw me, he sat on my bed, and to calm me started to pat me on my head and shoulders, like you do to an animal or child. He also tried to communicate with a few words, from which I gathered he wanted to know my age. I must say I was really stupid at 12 or 13, but we girls at that time were still children and kind of still believed in the "bird and bee" story and had no idea how babies were made, nor were we interested to know. But when it came to age, being the youngest I naturally wanted to be older so I told a lie and said "I was sixteen." The guy seemed pleased, and the patting and stroking my head and shoulders became a little stronger. Just at that minute, Papa returned with the little Mongolian, who had helped himself to anything of value. Papa was shocked to see what was going on, and to get the Russian away from me, he handed over whatever he thought would interest him: fountain pens, watches, alarm clocks, or whatever items the guy seemed to cast his eyes on. They finally left and Papa uttered a sigh of relief. But because he feared a repetition, he decided we females had to be put into hiding. Sadly, the first victorious ground troops - of any Nation - always feel they are entitled to help themselves to everything! Before the next arrival of any victors in our house, we were hidden in the broken shed adjoining the house, hoping the "raiders" would have no interest in investigating it.

It was early spring; the dampness of the ground where mattresses had been laid on made us--especially me--shiver. There was still fighting going on, but we realized that our town had been taken.

Chapter XV

A fter staying a few days in our hiding place being submitted to the dampness and cold, it was not surprising to Papa that I came down with a severe influenza and a high fever. He had no other choice but to move me back into the house. He put me in a room in the now vacant upstairs, and he hoped to frighten any of the Russian soldiers--in case they had any ideas regarding a young girl--by painting a big Red Cross on the door to indicate that I had a contagious disease. That seemed to work until one rainy day.

Our next door neighbors, an elderly married couple, lived in a grand mansion compared to ours that we thought was a really nice villa. This neighbor was an industrialist who, with a partner, had invented a procedure to line the inside of huge wine or beer tanks to stop any further fermentation. It had made him a very wealthy man. But despite that, they lived a very simple life, never seemed to entertain or have big parties.

Unfortunately for him and his wife, he must have joined the Nazi party when it was still illegal. These members were considered to have been the worst, and therefore had to expect the most severe consequences. Most likely, being a business man, our neighbor had been promised big advantages once Hitler would come into power. I think there were a lot like him who signed into the Nazi party for promised personal gains, and who were not really the diehard Nazis that caused so much devastation and misery.

With the Russian forces approaching, our unfortunate neighbor panicked and he and his wife took poison, which left their beautiful mansion open to the victors and the town "mob." Papa, being aware what was happening next door, had little hope that the Red Cross on the door would be enough to protect me.

I never forget this morning! Papa came into the room and said he was sorry having to do this to me! But I had to get up and-amidst the rain and fighting still going on in the surrounding hills-he quickly led me down to the end of our property. We had to duck every time we heard the hissing noise of the shrapnel flying over our heads.

The end of our property consisted of a part of the old town wall which goes back to medieval times. We kids used to call what was beyond that wall with an 8-foot drop, the "wolves' canon." It must have been one of Papa's hardest decisions to tell me that I had to jump down from this wall. He told me to hide in the shrubbery until the immediate danger was over, and he would come later and get me up with a ladder. Half stupid with fright, shivering in the rain, I thought the end of my days had come. To make me feel even worse was the crackling sound of dry branches breaking, as if somebody was searching for me. Thank God Papa finally arrived with the ladder. He said the danger was over for this time. The Russian soldiers had left disappointed for not having found what they had been looking for!

When I told Papa how frightened I was when I heard the crackling in the shrubs, he said that it was the caretaker's daughter that still lived at the mansion. Without any further explanation, he just said "she wasn't as lucky as you were to get away from them!"

Chapter XVI

Finally the war was officially over. Hitler with Eva Braun had committed suicide. Some of his high Ministers and Commanders not always successfully had tried to do the same. Most of them were captured and had to await judgment at the Nuremberg (Nuernberg) trial.

Although the war had ended, there was confusion and disorganization everywhere. Amazingly enough, I survived the adventure in the "Wolves Canon" without suffering a relapse. Sigrid, who had been worrying about Nicholas whether he was safe in Frankfurt, had a lovely surprise because all of a sudden he turned up one morning. How he got back from Frankfurt without any transport functioning was a miracle. To make it to his parent's place and then walk all the way where we lived was another achievement! That is why Papa was so fond of him. Nicholas certainly was no coward!

Now with Nicholas' support, Papa made a plan to make us safer. They decided to let a room upstairs completely disappear. Next to the bathroom was a door on a short wall that led into the next room. That wall with the door was hidden with wardrobes. The door on the other side of this room was opened but was made invisible from the adjoining room with Papa's big library cabinet from his downstairs study. How the two men got this heavy piece of furniture up the winding staircase was a true act of love. The beauty of this cabinet was that it had a kind of small niche on the bottom shelves where favorite books used to be ornamentally stacked. They cut the back of this niche to make it like a removable door so any of us could crawl in and out. When the camouflaging books were stacked into the niche, nobody could suspect that it led into another room.

We soon were able to set up "camp" with mattresses on the floor like a "community" bed. In the meantime one of my aunts with her live-in helper and her friend sought refuge in our family. Although we were somehow "prisoners," at least we were safe. The only one sometimes allowed out was Mama who tried to put a meal together for us from next to nothing in the way of supplies. Whenever uninvited Russian "visitors" appeared, Papa had to quickly get her back into our hideout. Once Mama had just managed to cook some dried beans (with dead beetles in some of them!!). Because she had to leave the pot on the kitchen table, one Russian took one spoonful and to show his disgust, spat right into the bean stew. I am sure their food was much more superior to ours!!! So after that, no bean stew for us! Nicholas had brought home two Frenchmen he met in the streets tramping between his parent's place and ours; there was still no transport.

Having two extra men for support was fine--except for Mama having to provide food for them as well. But Papa thought it looked kind of suspicious that there was a house of men without a woman!!! There was an older woman living opposite in the street from us that Papa thought would be the solution. She looked like one would imagine the appearance of a fortune teller wearing strange looking colorful clothes, her face painted with lots of makeup and golden chains of false jewelry around her neck. When Papa approached her to act as "lady of the house" in case we had "Russian alarm" she was delighted to accept. Next time these "visitors" came, she excitedly ushered them into the house, but the Russians took one look at her and left in a hurry, despite her effort to make them stay so that she could "entertain" them! When Papa told us the story, we at last had something to laugh about!

Chapter XVII

Slowly things seemed to settle down. The Russian soldiers were no longer allowed to roam around looking after their own personal interests and gains, because the now vacant beautiful mansion next door to us became the Russian headquarters. The commander was very strict and demanded obedience from his troops. Our city hall formed a kind of political party system with the Communist Party leading and the Democratic Socialists in pursuit. Papa, as I remember, had always been a Democrat, but he was smart enough not to "ruffle anybody's political feathers." He was highly respected, especially as he still was the only doctor! Having the Russian headquarters next door was in one way a blessing. But because we also had a nice villa, some of the officers rather fancied it for their quarters. Twice we were told to pack a small suitcase and leave, and it was only through the intervening head of the Communist Party that we could stay in our home. Another not so happy neighborly aspect was that the Russians started to raise pigs in the huge garage adjoining our house, and the poor pigs were not kept hygienically clean. The smell and flies in summer were terrible. And then, after one of the poor pigs ended up in their stomachs and having had too much vodka, poor Papa was called to tend to the "sick." Because our food supply had been poor for so long, Papa was skin and bones at that time, and certainly not used to eating fat pork. It is the Russian custom to be hospitable to a guest so, after being forced to eat pork and drink vodka in order not to offend them, Papa for days was on the sick list himself. Taking a stroll in our garden alone was also not to be recommended. Our neighbors just hopped over the wall when they felt like it.

Our cherries were another attraction for them. When a few soldiers once again entered over the wall and made it known they wanted some cherries, Papa invited them to help themselves. But they said: "No, you Papa!", meaning that Papa had to pick them. So Papa had to get up on the ladder himself to pick a basketful, while they watched him and laughed. In the evening, we had to get used to their Balalaika playing and loud singing, after obviously quite a few vodkas!

When fall arrived, high school opened up again. We were all glad that at last some kind of normality seemed to arrive for us. We had a new headmaster and many young new teachers. Most of the old classmates were there with some new ones as well. Boys and girls had classrooms on separate floors and the new headmaster made it clear that he meant "separate!" We were not supposed to mix! Seems kind of strange nowadays.

Vienna itself had been bombed quite severely in many parts, especially our beloved St. Stephan's Church and the Opera house, which were badly damaged. With most men away, either having fallen or taken prisoner, the women took it upon themselves and cleared the debris from the bombing and carted away wheelbarrows with sand and stones from the bomb-sites. Whoever proclaimed that women are the weaker sex should eat their words!

Chapter XVIII

When I met Petra again, I was glad to hear that she and her mother had also survived the first turbulent days unharmed under the protection of the priests in church. Petra was a grade higher from me, so we didn't see much of each other except in school. Papa's dream was that I would follow in his footsteps and become a doctor. I was quite sure that this was what I also wanted. Whenever his time permitted, he would take me in his surgery and give me a lecture like a university professor. I had to take notes and next time he would ask me questions to make sure that I understood the previous lesson. In these days, a doctor also conducted his own research into a patient's sickness--at least Papa did. That's probably why he had the reputation that his diagnosis was usually correct. He taught me how to obtain a urine sediment centrifugally or prepare other specimen by coloring them and putting them between two thin pieces of glass to be viewed under the microscope. I was fascinated to see what "dances" the now trapped bacteria were performing under the microscope. My interest pleased Papa, but he was less amused when Sigrid complained about my not obeying her instructions as my piano teacher. She said "I was fresh to her, rebellious, and not practicing as I should." Of course, she was right! I was entering puberty, and Sigrid was acting bossy and we were squabbling all the time. Not that I didn't want to learn; it was just opposing the way she used her authority. Papa had a cure for that; he simply said "Do you or don't you want to learn how to play the piano?" Naturally, I did want to learn! He probably talked to Sigrid as well, because suddenly we clicked and pretty soon Sigrid became so proud of me that she even arranged for her professor to hear me play. He was so impressed that he straight away wanted me to become his pupil at the Academy of Music, even without the usual entry exams by a panel of all the other professors. I was excited, but with now demanding highschool studies with new subjects like Latin, French, and more complicated Math and Physics, Papa flatly refused and that was that.

Despite our headmaster's strict separation rules, I discovered that boys could be quite nice, and boys discovered me also! With parental consent, a girlfriend and I were invited by two boys to see a musical in Vienna. It makes me smile when I think how innocent these first encounters with the opposite sex were!

Chapter XIX

Many changes started to take place. Although we were the 26th district (Bezirk) of Vienna under the Nazi regime, we now belonged to Lower Austria and were in the Russian zone. All the other three allies, especially the Americans, were not allowed to enter our zone, so we were "off limits" for them.

Vienna's now 23 districts were divided among the four allies: the Americans, British, Russians and French. The first district, the center of Vienna with its historical buildings, was declared to be under supervision of the four allies, with one of them taking charge monthly in a ceremonial military march and a symbolical exchange of the flag. Our own traffic police, called the "White Mice" because of the white caps of their uniform, proudly received some Harley Davidson motorbikes from the Americans as a gift.

To restore and maintain order, they also assisted the U.S. Military Police patrolling the streets and localities in their jeeps. To demonstrate the unity of the allies, you could sometimes see the four nations driving in a jeep together. In these days, I had no reason to leave my home grounds. At 15, I studied at our local high school, but of course always tried to find an excuse to see what was going on in Vienna itself. I heard rumors that there was a booming "black market" in one part where the American dollar was rated as being very desirable. This black market was the inspiration for the Hollywood movie "The Third Man," which was at that time filmed in Vienna.

The male stars were Orson Welles and Joseph Cotton; the pretty girl involved in that thriller was--I believe--Allida Valli, but my memory is not too clear about that. Our own Paul Hoerbiger played the janitor, and the "third-man-theme" performed on the zither by Anton Karas later became world famous.

Buying certain foods was still problematic, but the farmers across the Danube (Donau, our main stream) were self-sufficient and were happy to exchange their goods for desirable items they could not have afforded to buy. I think even during the war, this went on, but was forbidden and you had to be careful not to get caught. Seeing I was now a teenager, some of my childhood toys disappeared without my knowledge. I was very sad when I discovered my porcelain doll with her beautiful wardrobe had "departed" and the dollhouse Papa had made was also gone-- probably for a bag of potatoes and some speck (pork fat). Fortunately, my beloved teddy bear has survived and is still part of my life. I guess Mama knew better since the episode with my pet rabbit and my love for animals or anything resembling them.

Chapter XX

Nicholas had been successful applying for a position with the Vienna Philharmonic orchestra and became first flutist. We were all happy to have him stay in Vienna. Now that he had a secure and promising career, it wasn't long until wedding bells were in the air. I was to be Sigrid's bridesmaid and felt very important. The church wedding was to take place at our own beautiful historic church. The only problem was that the square in front of the entrance was open to all sides and therefore it was always very windy. Sigrid wore a lovely gown and I was supposed to carry her long veil. Well, the gusty wind took hold of the veil, and in order to prevent Sigrid from being "air-lifted," I did my utmost to hold the veil to the ground. I guess that must have pulled the way it was fastened to her hair, and in true sisterly fashion, she turned around and verbally gave me a piece of her mind! "Well," I thought "Thank God I won't have to put up with that much longer now that she is married!"

It was a lovely wedding and following reception dinner, and everybody toasted the happy couple. Their departure to their new home on top of the Vienna woods was very romantic in a horse drawn carriage. As I waved them "good-bye," I couldn't help feeling a little sad, but I knew I would soon visit Sigrid for my piano lesson and Nicholas had mentioned he had a cat and dog that I couldn't wait to play with. I now appreciated Sigrid's teaching and she also had become quite proud of my progress.

Somehow the house seemed very quiet without Sigrid, but school became more demanding and didn't leave much time for sadness. I got on well with my schoolmates, but I was unhappy that Petra, who was a grade higher, left school at the end of the year to start work at a jeweler's shop in the center of Vienna. So it was inevitable that we drifted apart.

In summer I and my friends went to the beach nearly every day which was on a dead sidearm of the Danube, and many city people from Vienna also spent their weekends and summer vacations there. It was almost a small "holiday city" consisting of very nicely built summer houses. There were also restaurants, a swimming pool with shower facilities, two sundecks and a big square with benches that was a meeting place for young and old. My friends and I took full advantage of that. I had noticed that some members of the opposite sex were quite attractive! Especially one young guy that my girlfriends knew seemed to fall into this category.

Not unlike young puppies, we were constantly teasing and wrestling with one another. This young man also seemed to have noticed that the opposite sex had certain attractions. In one of these wrestling matches he dragged me behind some bushes, and I discovered that being kissed by a guy can be quite pleasant. That was the beginning of my first experience of "falling in love." We exchanged friendship rings and it was accepted by our friends that we were a "couple." Naturally, my boyfriend had to be a good dancer who could do all the new American dance forms. But, like most "first loves," it didn't last. I was a fun-loving girl and quite popular, so mistrust set in. Strangely enough, I think neither of us got completely over it, and even much later in life, there were one or two occasions when the old feelings could have been rekindled. But today it just remains a sweet memory.

Chapter XXI

I always made friends with older--to my mind--sophisticated girls. After school on our way home, my new girlfriend Sylvie always came up to my room to have a cigarette because she wasn't allowed to smoke at home. In all the Hollywood movies everybody seemed to smoke. Sylvie looked like she really could compete handling smoking cigarettes as elegantly like any of these Hollywood actors. I was fascinated and asked her for a cigarette. I felt very grown up puffing on my first cigarette. Sylvie was not impressed and said I looked ridiculous. "You must inhale the smoke, not just puff it," she informed me. My pride was hurt so, after she left, I decided to put in some practice. I knew Papa wasn't home and, being a smoker himself, would probably have some cigarettes laying about. So I went downstairs to investigate. I found an open packet of "Camel," American cigarettes that one of his patients probably had given him as a "thank-you" gift. Most likely it came from the "Black Market" that a GI had sold for Austrian shillings, so he could take his girlfriend out to a local café.

I thought Papa wouldn't notice one cigarette missing, so I took one. Again in my room, I lit the cigarette and started to practice "inhaling." One successful draw and the room started spinning around. I thought I was passing out or dying and had to lay down. I observed "puffing" seemed a lot less dangerous! But next time Sylvie came, I wanted to show off and bravely asked for a cigarette. Sylvie looked at me doubtfully and must have thought I was going to waste another of her precious cigarettes "puffing" away! But, unbelievably, the inhaling worked, probably because the Austrian cigarettes were not as strong! That was the beginning of 19 years of smoking; thank goodness I stopped in time!!

Next time Sigrid and Nicholas came visiting, Nicholas offered me a cigarette in front of Papa, because he had seen me smoke before at their house. With raised eyebrows, Papa took notice that I could already inhale, shook his head and called me a "silly goose." He himself realized how bad it was to be "hooked." To prevent me from making my own cigarettes using cigarette-butt tobacco from his used cigarette ends, he awarded me one packet of cigarettes a week. But between Sylvie and myself, it never lasted very long!

Sylvie lived in the next township; you could take a bus, but it wasn't so far that you couldn't get there by walking. She asked me to come and meet me at the café there because she had a date with a guy she didn't care for very much. This café was a popular meeting place. I agreed and Sylvie's date didn't seem to mind that I also had turned up. We listened to the latest hits on the radio and smoked while Sylvie's date ordered drinks. We had quite a nice time. It was the middle of winter. All of a sudden, the door swung open, and at least eight or ten guys came marching in. The one in front was a gorgeous looking guy in ski gear who seemed to have popped out of a sports fashion magazine. Everybody was excited and they all knew one another. I was like the "new kid on the block." Before I knew what was happening, this handsome guy sat next to me. He had just won a ski race on the surrounding steep hills. Naturally more drinks were ordered to celebrate "Toni's" victory, and I was being asked where I had been "hiding" for so long. I got extremely nervous with Toni looking at me with eyes that were like those of a beautiful cat or tiger. I had never seen green eyes with a sparkle like his. Sylvie could see that I was uneasy; the radio provided no more music, so she asked me to play the latest hits on the piano. But Toni followed me even to the piano. By now, everybody had a few drinks and applauded my "hit parade." It was getting late and when I asked what time it was, I was told that the last bus was gone. Well, Toni offered to see that I got home safely!!! With all the drinks we had, the goodnight kiss got a little more passionate than it should have, so I knew that there was a real man behind it. Something inside told me that I should put a safety device into motion and not see this guy again! This was not just like falling in love; it was the danger of falling too deeply! We did make a date, but I hoped I would be strong enough not to keep it! Next day when I talked to Sylvie and told her about the way I felt, she was shocked and quite beside herself! She told me Toni and his family had a terrible reputation with drinking and brawls. Yes, Toni was a nice guy liked by all, especially the girls! But look out if you crossed him. He would turn into a tiger. Yes, I could understand Sylvie's warning, but- oh - why did Toni have to be so handsome and have this exciting air about himself that made me feel the way I did? However, I promised myself not to turn up at the date with Toni.

Chapter XXII

My mind was still in turmoil whether or not I should keep my date with Toni. Even Sylvie could not help me with this decision when I visited her. She lived in the same neighboring town where we had met in the café the other day. The memory of all this came back to me while I was waiting for the bus to take me home. I couldn't believe my eyes when the center of my indecision came walking right out the door of the barber shop opposite the bus station. My heart missed a couple of beats because when he saw me, he walked straight over to me. He seemed pleased that we met again so soon and invited me for coffee or a drink. Naturally, I couldn't refuse and didn't catch the bus!!!

In the following weeks, we met many times. It was fun, but also disturbing not knowing how he really felt about me. One of his friends dated Sylvie, so the four of us often did crazy things together.

Toni's attitude puzzled me. When we were together, he acted as if he was in love with me, but I heard that he was also taking out other girls. So, what is a female's strategy to solve this unnerving situation?? My intuition told me to let him have a taste of his own behavior and provide him with some competition! The "Fortis" were the time of the "Big Band Era." Jazz and the new American dance styles had taken all young people---including me--by storm. Sylvie loved dancing the same as I did, so we followed a certain band whenever we could. At one dance a trumpet player and the band leader had asked Sylvie and me to wait until the dance was over and they had packed up their instruments. We were flattered and--of course--we waited! The trumpet player--his name was Erik--was a very well mannered young man; he actually studied at the same Music Academy like Sigrid. Although studying classical music, most of the young guys there also occasionally played in jazz bands to make some extra money. My parents approved of Erik, so whenever he played at a dance, I was allowed to attend, providing he would escort me home late at night. This suited me beautifully. I could dance while poor Erik had to watch me having fun. During intermission he would come down from the stage and sit with me, and I was the envy of the other girls because jazz musicians were like Hollywood idols.

I liked Erik but was not in love with him like I was with Toni. However, my strategy seemed to work. It wasn't long until Toni heard about it and all of a sudden his attitude changed! At last he spoke of his love for me and things got a lot more serious!! Poor Erik, who really seemed to care about me, was heartbroken. Today I deeply regret that I have misused Erik's affection for my own calculating scheme! Most likely that would result in bad karma for the future! But at the time, I brushed my scruples aside. I had to deal with preparation for the final exams so I could be admitted to University to become a doctor. The exams were nerve racking, but thank goodness I passed.

Chapter XXIII

U nfortunately, my happiness didn't last very long because Papa must have heard that my involvement with Toni wasn't altogether an innocent one. Papa was a very respected member of our community, and his youngest daughter was closely watched by "well meaning" older citizens!!! Not knowing what to make of it, he delegated Mama, who questioned me with a serious face, what was behind the rumors. I could never lie to Mama and admitted that I had fallen for Toni. Papa, who not only was disappointed in me but also shocked about Toni's bad reputation and family background, gave me the ultimatum to either give him up and start University to become a doctor or to get myself a job.

Giving up Toni was impossible, and for the first time, I saw Papa almost crying from disappointment and frustration. So---what to do next? I had always been interested in fashion; I liked to draw and make some of my clothes, which gave me the idea to apply at a Fashion House for the position as a "Designer." When the boss asked for my qualifications, he was not impressed and said he couldn't expect his designers to teach me the profession. I should attend a Fashion School and he might then give me another chance. I was devastated and went to see my Aunt Louise who had always been very understanding. After taking her into my confidence, she decided she would take a critical look at Toni and judge for herself what he was like. Well, when I presented Toni to her, he was most charming and instantly won Aunt

Louise's heart. Being the resolute person she was, she marched to see Papa and took up battle with him. I had told her about my failed job interview and that I had been advised to attend a Fashion School. That was what the loud arguing with Papa was all about. Aunt Louise won and Papa agreed he would let me have my way.

I was euphoric when I passed the talent test and was admitted at the most prestigious Fashion School in Vienna.

Chapter XXIV

Neither Papa nor I had realized that becoming a Designer at that school would take five years! I wonder if it occurred to Papa that for the amount of time and financial outlay, I might as well have gone to University with a medical doctor's degree!! But here I was at the Fashion School, which was situated in a former historic "hunting castle" close to the old Monarchy's residence "Schoenbrunn" and a beautiful park surrounding it. How exciting it was to walk the grounds where once illustrious Royal guests had been entertained.

Our first 2 years were spent mainly in learning via drawing lessons the relationship of the human figure to fashion. Our tastes were refined; color combinations and making artifacts from paper were also important in our training. Year three you could choose your specialty. You could major in hand weaving, fabric print design, dressmaking, jewelry, millinery or accessories.

I chose dressmaking, which really is fashion designing. Other subjects included were languages, knowledge of fabrics, commercial arithmetic, plus a thrilling end-of-each- year grand fashion parade and exhibition. The media built up the parade in the park to a great event, where the first basic classes paraded historical costumes made from crepe-paper basted onto calico, and the dressmaker classes modeled their own designs on the catwalk. I really enjoyed being part of it!!

The only drawback was the 90 minute travel time each way

changing from bus to multiple trams (trolleys). Summertime was no problem, but in winter it was agony to wait for the bus or trams to arrive. School hours were from 8 in the morning to 5 in the afternoon, so in winter it meant leaving and arriving home in the dark. I had made friends with another girl who traveled on the same route, except for the bus. Her name was Ilona, Loni for short. We shared the same table in school and became good "buddies." Toni sometimes picked me up after school and I felt very "special." We often talked about our future together, which-because of Papa's opposition-did not look very rosy. I was shocked when Toni told me that he had applied for a 2-year contract erecting ready-made houses in Australia! With the money saved, he would either send for me or return so we could get married. I was touched about his initiative, but couldn't imagine 2 years without Toni!

But the ball was rolling and the time to part came all too soon! Toni, when he saw me home for the last time, did not give me a chance to break into tears, a last hug, a kiss, and I was left standing there alone...!

Chapter XXV

In all the turmoil of events in my life, nothing else seemed to be of significant importance.

Yes, I was happy for Carla when Fred proposed to her and formally asked Papa for his consent for their marriage.

Yes, I was very happy when Sigrid and Nicholas became parents. But I was depressed without Toni and felt very much alone like living on an island by myself.

Papa, who probably had heard of Toni's departure, even started talking to me again. Maybe he thought that Toni's absence would cure me of my infatuation! How wrong he was!

I could think of nothing else but my loneliness, and the short postcard from Genua before embarking on the vessel taking him to Australia, did nothing to cheer me up. Loni, at school, eyed me suspiciously and asked: "Was I going to be like that forever and become old and wrinkled before my time?" I sensed that she was becoming impatient with me, so I finally gave in when she insisted that I should meet some of her friends. It did help to break my isolation, and eventually I quite enjoyed meeting them now and then. Loni was happy to see the change in me, and I agreed when she suggested to take a stroll after school to go "window shopping" in the elegant streets of Vienna. Before that, I hadn't really noticed that the Center City was full of activity. Many of the American soldiers (GI's) that were the occupying forces after the war, used their off-duty time to get acquainted with what Vienna had to offer! Naturally they also looked for female company!! They all looked handsome and clean-cut in their uniforms, quite different from what we were used to seeing in the Russian zone where Loni and I lived. It wasn't long when we noticed that we were being followed by two of these handsome guys. Loni, who was happy that I had finally "joined the world again," got into an adventurous mood and decided we should side-track them for a bit of fun. I got quite worried where this was going to lead, but Loni just dragged me along and told me not to be a spoil-sport! So we criss-crossed in all the small side streets and when we turned the next corner, the same two guys stood in front of us. They must have realized our tactics and probably enjoyed playing "hide and seek." Loni seemed to be completely at ease and readily accepted their invitation for coffee in the small café nearby. I was tongue-tied and nervous and could hardly put my "school-English" into words. Loni chatted away happily and it seemed that her new acquaintance wanted to meet her again. He didn't know when he would be off-duty again, so Loni gave him my phone number to arrange a date. I was a bit worried because Papa's phone was only so patients could contact him, and we were not allowed to use it, unless it was an emergency. Was Loni's date an emergency???

But, fortunately, the phone call came when Papa wasn't home and I was back from school. When I asked Loni's new friend when he wanted to see her, the answer was "I don't want to meet Loni; I want to see you; I'm the other guy!" Well, that was a surprise! Although Toni was still on my mind, he hadn't written for so long and I was very disappointed in him. This young American seemed very nice; he was tall and handsome--and I could improve my English!!! So--why not?! Also, meeting him in Vienna would be away from the eyes of the "gossip-brigade" in our town!

My first date with "Vincent," Vince for short, was very pleasant, and Loni was happy that her dates with "Gery" could be arranged with the help of Vince, because they served in the same company. At last, life seemed much brighter, and Loni and I had many exciting things to talk about!!!

Chapter XXVI

P apa and Mama enjoyed their new status as "grandparents." Carla and Fred had a quiet civil wedding, nothing elaborate like Sigrid's. Mama had talked Papa into letting the newlyweds occupy the first floor, and I also was to have a room upstairs. Fred had opened up his law practice, but didn't have many clients at first. To help with their budget, Carla decided to keep working until Fred had established a reliable clientele and income. Nicholas quite often was on tour with the Philharmonic orchestra and Sigrid had put her career as a pianist on hold, being a mother to her son André. I often stayed at Sigrid's house overnight after a date with Vince. I still had my piano lessons with Sigrid, although I didn't have much time to practice. I could also take Vince there because they lived in the American zone. When I introduced Vince to Nicholas, his comment was: "A nice guy, but he's a country boy!" Well, I didn't know anything about America in these days; to me it was all big and wonderful with the best jazz musicians in the world!!! How was I to know that Iowa was a rural state?! Loni questioned me how our romance was progressing? I had nothing to report other than that Vince was a kind and courteous guy, and that at last we had kissed "good-bye" when he escorted me to the train station.

She certainly had more exciting news! She said the guys had decided to lease a room in a private house so that we could have more privacy! I bet that this had been Gery's idea, who seemed to really be in love with Loni. I thought I would wait till I would hear it from Vince. Yes, the kissing got much more intense and we had fallen in love. Toni was far away and most likely had another girl so when Vince asked "Did I want to go to the room?" I agreed. It was in a beautiful old Viennese building, and I was glad it wasn't in a hotel. We were both a bit embarrassed so we just talked for a while, hugged and kissed. Vince didn't rush me, spoke of his love for me, and that he thought of re-enlisting because he would be shipped home to America very soon. When I asked why he wanted to re-enlist, he said "because he thought he wanted to marry me!"

Well, that wasn't exactly a proposal, but good enough for another round of kisses--and, yes, we did become "Lovers."

Chapter XXVII

With Toni being out of the picture, Papa and I had a much better relationship. It was the end of the school year when the works of some pupils were displayed. Papa had never been to the school before, but he agreed to come and let me show him around.

I have had a good year, and Papa was very proud to see that I was present in nearly every subject in the exhibition. Another big factor for his happiness was his two-year-old grandson André. He was a dear little fellow and Papa doted on him whenever his time allowed. Loni's romance blossomed and Gery had even bought her an engagement ring. She told me they would get married before Gery--the same as Vince--would be shipped back home to the U.S. at the end of their enlisted time. Nothing like that was happening with me and Vince. I thought less and less of Toni who had not written in a long time. Knowing him, he probably had found a new love in Australia.

Nicholas and Sigrid often gave parties, mainly because Nicholas enjoyed entertaining his musician friends. Sigrid, on the other hand, liked to surround herself with her former colleagues--and even her professor from the Academy. I used to bring Vince and he quite enjoyed himself too.

But like all happy times in life, it wasn't meant to last. In the following year, Papa became unwell, often had a fever and--though he consulted some specialists who suspected various reasons--no one came up with a diagnosis. Perhaps Papa was the only one who knew he was doomed.

Carla was nearing the end of her pregnancy when Papa became so ill that he had to close his practice and was admitted into our local hospital. Mama stayed with Papa day and night only to rush home to cook something for him because he could not digest the hospital food. I now wish that I had been more supportive for Mami! But, although I was worried over Papa's illness, my head was so full with my own problems! One day, on my way home from school, I bought a bunch of violets for Papa as a reminder that spring was around the corner. Papa was pleased to see me, but when I suggested that he would soon come home, he sadly shook his head. He made me promise that whatever life demanded of me, I would always give my very best! In all the years after his passing, I tried very hard to honor my promise to him. Vince was very sweet next time we met and dried my tears. After the ordeal of the funeral, a letter from Toni arrived out of the blue. He wrote he had saved enough money for my sea-fare, he liked Australia and wanted me to join him so we could get married!! That letter really unnerved me! Now I was sitting between two chairs! I desperately wanted to belong to somebody. I felt alone, with everybody being busy with their own lives. Was the old bond with Toni still strong enough to risk spending a lifetime with him, and why had Vince not said anything about his plans for our future?! The time for a decision arrived on our last night together, when Vince said nothing about his intentions. I could not stand this uncertainty any longer, so I told Vince that I planned to immigrate to Australia to get married. He looked shocked with--maybe--just a hint of relief because he did not have to make a decision! Knowing his horoscope in the sign of "Cancer," it showed me that he was a true "Cancerian," taking one step forward and two backward!!! He wished me all the best and expressed the hope that we somehow could stay in touch. I was sad that my relationship with him hadn't worked as it had for

Loni. I had always felt safe in Vince's company, and I was sure he would have made a good husband.

When I told Mami about my plans to join Toni, she accepted it like the unselfish mother she was, hoping it would bring me happiness.

Chapter XXVIII

Time ran away so fast for us that walking out of the beautiful castle that had been our school, came all too soon. We knew that this was the last time! We still would have had another year before graduation but due to our circumstances, we left with the blessing of the director.

Toni had sent me all the application forms for the Australian visa and there was a lot to do. The worst was that I was required to be vaccinated against smallpox, which Papa had always avoided. Most vaccination sera are based on eggs, and I was allergic to them. But the Australian government insisted on it, so I had to comply. Ten days before I was supposed to catch the train to Genua to embark the ocean liner for my journey to Australia, I became violently ill with a high fever. I was given Quinine in the hope that I would be well enough to leave. Luckily, I made it!!

The morning came when Mami and Carla, who now had a baby son Karl, walked me to the railway station. Mami smiled bravely, but I had trouble holding back my tears! My feeling of excitement was mixed with anxiety and a slight bit of fear what the future might bring.

In the train compartment other people were also traveling for the same reason as I, so I felt a bit more secure in their company. The sight of the beautiful huge Italian vessel "The Australia" as she lay docked in the harbor was overwhelming that I could hardly wait to set foot on. I almost felt as if I was acting in a movie, when this moment finally arrived. My cabin was in Tourist class that I shared with three other women; one of them was the lady I had met on the train. After we settled in, we were summoned to the dining room that was abuzz with excited people. The food was delicious and typically Italian with Antipasto, a pasta entree before the main course, dessert and various cheeses to finish and--naturally--plenty of red wine. After dinner, most of us went up on deck to watch the crew prepare for departure.

It was a heart wrenching experience when the moment came and I saw Europe slowly disappear through a haze of tears --and too much wine!! The following 3 weeks were like living on another planet, watching the activities when we stopped at foreign ports. During the day we could swim in the pool, play games on deck, or just be lazy in the sun. At night there was dancing or you could watch a movie. One day we even had a storm that really "rocked the boat!" Many people were sea-sick and one had to be careful when stepping into the lift in case somebody had been sea-sick in there.

We finally reached our last port which was Fremantle before reaching our final destination at Melbourne. My excitement was really building up: How would Toni act? In my romantic fantasy, I pictured him taking me in his arms and whispering into my ear: "Oh, my darling, here you are at last! I will never let you go again!"

Chapter XXIX

T he disembarking procedures took far too long for my impatience, so sadly the meeting with Toni turned out quite different from what I had hoped for. Yes, he gave me a hug, but remarked that I should have written from our last port (Fremantle)!!! Was that the welcome of a lover being reunited with the love of his life?!

The next disappointment came when after a few days, he scolded me for spending money buying a cheap lipstick in a store. I realized that my life wasn't going to be easy. I appreciated that he had used up his savings for my sea-fare and I understood that the added responsibility for me made him nervous. I knew the going would be tough!

Toni had rented a room with sharing a kitchen and bathroom. The "landlord" was a grouchy man who picked on the way I did things at every opportunity. That caused much friction between Toni and me. I hoped I would soon be able to find a job so that I could contribute to our budget. But first we had to get married! Toni, with his charm, had successfully founded a "one man" painting and decorating business and was well liked by his clients. Some of them even came to our wedding and gave us a reception. Sadly, Toni drank too much and our "wedding night" was a complete washout!

Now that he thought he owned me body and soul, he didn't seem concerned whenever he hurt me. Afterwards, there were always promises that "it would never happen again!" But, of course, he never kept these promises so I could never feel completely at ease. My pride prevented me from confiding to friends or family in Austria.

Sitting alone in our room waiting for Toni to come home in the evening drove me crazy. It was time to look for a job!!! With my training, I thought I was well equipped to land a top position. But every time I went for an interview, the refrain was always the same: "Where did you work before?" At last, I was accepted at a dressing gown firm, and when I was asked if I knew how to use a "cutter," I naturally thought they meant a pair of scissors. So I said "yes." To my surprise, I was handed a small "cutting machine" with a mean looking circular blade. The head cutter lady told me to lay up an amount of collar interlinings and then to cut them out with the electric cutting machine. Bravely, I started it but the fabric pulled into the rapidly turning blade. In my effort to stop a "catastrophe" by ruining all the fabric, my left index finger got caught in the blade and it went halfway through the cap of my finger. Afraid to lose my first job, I made my way to the bathroom leaving a trail of blood behind! The factory manager found me there and sent me home. To my surprise, I wasn't fired! I realized I had a lot to learn because we were not trained for mass production in our wonderful school!

Many other accidents happened, like: when I cut through the electric cord and the resulting sparks sent me on a high jump that could have won me an Olympic medal! Even more dramatic was the time when I was allowed to use the big cutter with the straight blade moving rapidly up and down, which was used for high fabric lays of 20 or 30 garments. Nobody had told me that there was a difference into which receptacle the electric cord had to be plugged in. Well, it was the wrong one and I caused a "short" in the whole factory! The two bosses were running around as if we had been attacked by an enemy. All the sewing machines were "dead" and the girls operating them were on piece work and thus lost all their daily profit! I thought it wise to sneak out the back way when going home so I wouldn't have to face them cursing me!

It's a wonder that my two bosses, who were tough businessmen, didn't fire me! Even when I was told for the first time to lay out the pattern pieces of a garment and sketch them into the fabric, and it took me a lot more fabric than the designer had estimated, I still didn't lose my job! From then on, whenever there was fabric missing, I heard the bosses say: "Of course, Melanie always takes an extra yard!!" Well, I soon learned that there was to be no space between the garment pieces (think of it like a jigsaw puzzle) and when I finally reached my goal to be a designer in charge, I earned the respect of the cutting department because I had been through a tough training myself!

Chapter XXX

My two bosses started to recognize my progress and made me "head-cutter." Really, I should have been pleased, especially when I also got a little more money, but there was nothing more that I could learn as a "cutter."

I decided that I was ready for a designing position. I thought I might as well start at the top! An evening gown firm was looking for a designer, so I went for an interview. The lady in charge seemed to like me, but when I mentioned that I could also make dress patterns, she raised her eyebrows and said "that was expected of me!" She led me to a small room which was to be my office. I was given a picture of an evening gown with a chart of measurements and then I was on my own. In Vienna, we were taught to first draft a base pattern according to given measurements, and from this the required pattern for the design was developed.

After 2 hours the lady came back to see how I was doing. When I proudly displayed only a sleeve pattern and very few additional pieces, she said "to leave everything" and come to her office. She handed me $2.00-and that was it. Not experienced enough!!! A hard pill to swallow, especially when I had to confess it to Toni. Well, back to learning more lessons! With my experience as a cutter, I had no problem finding another job. This time, however, I was going to keep my eyes open regarding pattern making. I found out that every firm has already established base patterns in the size required. So that eliminated valuable time. I watched and learned. When I discovered all I wanted to know, I quit. I think that year I changed jobs 10 times! I remember when I had started a job in the morning, I gave notice to the boss in the afternoon! He was puzzled and asked "why?" I couldn't very well tell him that there was nothing of interest in his business that I could learn anything from! My first designing jobs were mainly for blouses that didn't require making elaborate patterns. As I gained experience, I felt I was ready to really start my career as a "Designer."

During the "fifties", Melbourne had a booming fashion industry and every firm had their own resident designer. If you were good, the word soon got around in the trade, and behind the scenes you were frequently offered a better position (with more money!) by a competing firm. A successful designer often got recommended by representatives of fabric and accessories(like buttons and belts) because a top designer would bring more business for them also. I always thought that the fashion trade was very much like show business with its good and bad features. I had a wonderful job at the time, when a letter came from one of Toni's cousins in Austria. She wanted to come to Australia and asked if she could stay with us. We had just bought our first house and started to renovate it. So, of course, we said she would be welcome.

I liked the girl, but Toni--who could never handle emotional stress without alcohol-- started to drink more. When the cousin came, she had a letter of recommendation for a job with a German firm, but it was too far from where we lived. However, she was able to rent a room closer to her work. Toni's birthday came, and we invited her to stay with us over the weekend so we could celebrate. But she called and made an excuse: "She had to do something for work." Toni was disappointed but accepted it.

In the middle of the night, the phone rang. It was from a hospital saying that the cousin had met with an accident crossing the busy highway when she made that phone call to us. In the excitement, Toni didn't understand whether she had already died or whether the doctors were fighting for her life. Toni took off in the car like a madman, leaving me in shock. Well, she had died and we could do nothing but call Toni's father so he could tell the sad news to her parents. It was a nightmare that couldn't have been worse! After we had taken care of funeral arrangements and sending her remains home to her parents, Toni insisted he wanted to be with his family. I could understand that, but we had just gotten on our feet with our first real home, I had a good job and planned to look after everything until his return. But, no! I had to quit my wonderful job; the house and everything else had to be sold at a loss. And off we went to Europe!!

Chapter XXXI

It was not a happy homecoming! Even in my family, where we stayed, many changes had taken place. Nicholas and Sigrid were divorced, but both had remarried. Sigrid, her new husband "Simon" and young André had moved into Papa's surgery that Sigrid had turned into a small apartment. She was quite a "handyman." Carla's marriage was on "rocky grounds," and when it came to Toni and me, I could not honestly say that we lived in "marital bliss." He was drinking more again, sometimes not even coming home until the next day! Naturally I thought he was staying with his family. Mama had moved upstairs with Carla so that we could have her apartment. My family had become aware of my situation but when I cried, Mama said quite rightly: "You wanted him, and you got him." Toni was not a good influence on teenager André either. He even gave him alcohol at times. He upset the whole family and our arguments did not help. It must have been a relief for everybody when we moved out to stay with Toni's father. It was no relief for me though!! Toni's father reacted exactly like Toni when it came to handling emotional stress. They both believed in alcohol as a remedy. Now I also found out where he had been staying when he didn't come home! It was with his childhood girlfriend! I knew her from high school days and being naive, always thought their friendship was strictly about memories of fun days that we all have from carefree times in our youth. I even tried to become part of that friendship with her but never got a response.

Half of the time I didn't know where Toni was, so I paid my old fashion school a visit. I was given a tour of all the classrooms and was treated like a VIP because "I was a successful designer in Australia!" It was kind of sentimental to meet some of my old teachers and walk on familiar ground. I restrained myself from advising them to put more emphasis on training the pupils for the tough world of mass production. Only very few would ever make it into "High Fashion" (Haute Couture) in Paris or other fashion metropolis where specialized people would make the dress patterns for their designs. The visit was very pleasant and brought back memories. I wondered how Loni's venture to the U.S. had turned out and hoped that she was happy!

The situation was escalating to an unbearable stage! My employers in Australia wanted me back, so one morning when Toni reappeared, I confronted him that I had decided to fly back to Australia and he could stay! I think he was so shocked that he accepted my decision. Before I departed, I went to say goodbye to my family and paid a last visit to the cemetery to say goodbye to Papa.

I was so disappointed with what I once thought was a great love, that I wished Toni would remain in Austria and let me rebuild my own life. But--it wasn't long until he was on the way back to Melbourne, sober and full of good intentions. So we had to start all over again, work and save money until we could afford a down payment for another house. In the meantime, we lived in a rented apartment. The opportunity for another house arrived through a realtor friend. It was pretty rundown but in an excellent location close to shopping and the beach. With Toni's expertise in the contractor business, we soon remodeled it into a delightful house that had a Mediterranean look. The small rooms were transformed into an open living area with archways instead of doors, except for the master bedroom and bathroom.

Life seemed to start looking better for us. Unfortunately, this optimistic outlook didn't last very long. Politics in the government changed with the next election and the fashion industry especially suffered a heavy blow. No manufacturer could afford a resident designer anymore; they only needed the original garment design with the pattern and all garments were produced in countries where labor was cheap, unless some manufacturers specialized in only making up (sewing the precut garments).

Most designers--including myself--went into "freelancing." I started to work from home, which did not please Toni because nearly all the people I worked for were men. I guess he judged me by his own standard and always suspected me of infidelity. Anybody who knows how tough it is at collection time, when fashion houses want to show their new designs to buyers, will be aware that designers have to work around the clock when everybody wants their work done "like yesterday!" Besides, any romantic involvement with the boss is soon public knowledge in the trade! So it is not to be recommended! The fact that I earned a lot of money was no objection for Toni, but he felt that I was neglecting him. So he started again to drink more. He resented some of the people I worked for coming to the house and, sometimes, was even quite rude to them. Fortunately, people liked my work enough to put up with it. My salvation came when a friend in the fashion business told me there was a vacancy of a room in a fashionable building in the city, where clients could come to see me. To my surprise, Toni agreed and I took up residence in my "studio," had business cards and stationary printed, and my business flourished in due course.

Chapter XXXII

I'll never be able to forget this day! I was in the middle of a conference with one of my clients when a telegram arrived from Carla: "Mama had suffered a massive heart attack!" I raced home but Toni was at work. I could not waste any time and booked the next flight available to Vienna. Toni was not happy, but this was an emergency that he had to accept. Carla picked me up from the airport; it was a sad drive home! Funeral arrangements had already been made, and I felt kind of numb as if I wasn't able to accept reality. Mami had not left a will, so my two sisters and I all inherited a third of the property. Although Fred and Carla were separated, Fred-- being a lawyer--took care of all legal business. Before long, I was on the plane again to face up to my responsibilities. I think I once read that you only really grow up when your Mother is no longer here. Well, I sadly felt very grown-up at this moment!

I must have been fantasizing when I expected any sympathy from Toni on my return.

No, if anything, he blamed me for leaving him, and that I always consider myself more important than him! His job requests from people had declined because his breath always smelled from alcohol, and therefore people hesitated to hire him. My own career was the opposite. I was more and more in demand! Two of the Fashion houses I worked for wanted me on their premises part-time also, so I was busier than ever. At work I tried not to think about my situation at home and acted bright and positive, but when I raced home to cook dinner, the full impact of my misery hit me. Toni, who had been sitting home drinking without food, was abusive and waiting for a chance to attack me. I tried to put food in front of him as quickly as I could, but by that time he didn't want it any more, swiped the plate off the table and usually I had to run for my life, walking the streets without having eaten myself! The worst time came when I was approached by an important client to fly to Paris and London on his behalf, to check out new fashion trends. I guess at first Toni was flattered when I told him--that his wife was so important and he agreed that I should accept. But when I did, and told him so in the evening, he became a raving maniac. He had been violent and beat me before, but this time he even hit out at furniture and once again I had to run for my life. Although this was clearly "domestic violence," the police did not want to get involved! I spent the night at a girlfriend's place, and I knew I had to make a decision! Fortunately, Toni was not home in the morning, so I gathered what I needed plus my passport, loaded up my car and looked for an apartment in another suburb. I also went to a lawyer and filed for divorce. The whole day was spent on the phone, and I felt desperately alone. But that was nothing new, and several times I thought about Vince and regretted my impatience at the time. How different my life could have been with him. I still had his phone number, so at the spur of the moment I called him. I knew that he also had married so in case his wife answered, I would just hang up. But, no, it was Vince that answered! How good it was to hear his voice! When I asked him if he was still married, he said "no." His wife had died. After telling him of my misery and that I was being sent on a mission to Europe, I told him of my marital situation that I had left my husband and filed for divorce. He was shocked and very sympathetic. I also mentioned that I was flying to Europe within a week. Vince promised to call me the next day at my studio to find out how I was making out. That night I slept in my new surrounding not only from exhaustion, but also because somebody far away was thinking of me!

The phone call from Vince the next day brought another surprise to lift my spirit! He said he always had wanted to visit Europe again and would I mind if he accompanied me?! Would I mind??? I was ecstatic at the prospect to see Vince again so soon! Part of my contract to take this trip was that I could stay a week with my family in Austria before London and Paris.

So Vince would meet me in Vienna and we would then arrange to fly together where I had to carry out my mission. I could hardly wait and everything I had been through became like a nightmare that I had survived . . .

Chapter XXXIII

After being in Vienna for 2 days, the long awaited moment finally arrived. Carla and I were on the way to the airport to pick up Vince. How will he look after all these years, how will he react when he sees me, had I been right in fantasizing that he was the true love that my youthful impatience had driven away??? Once at the airport nervousness really set in. I could hardly stand still waiting at the "arrival gate." At last, the first people started to come through. It was an emotionally charged atmosphere. After all, I wasn't the only one waiting for somebody "special." I felt like I was playing a part in a romantic movie! When Vince saw me, he hurried toward me, dropped his travel bags on the floor and took me in his arms. He held me as if he never wanted to let go of me again! The next week we were like a couple of teenagers in love. Vince told me that he often thought of me, although he had a good marriage and mourned after losing his wife to a fatal illness.

After the happy days filled with the excitement of our reunion, I had to face the reality of my job mission--a week in Paris and then another one in London. My instruction was to investigate all the shopping streets and stores for new trends. Poor Vince, not being used to such a lot of vigorous walking, was simply exhausted. Americans are used to getting in and out of their cars wherever they wanted to go! He said he had no idea that the fashion trade was so strenuous! Little did he know that this was like a holiday compared to the real work involved being a Fashion Designer! But at least all this walking built up Vince's appetite and this caused our first disagreement. He wanted to look for "McDonalds" and a juicy "hamburger" whereas I wanted to have a taste of real "French cuisine." However, Vince eventually approved of a beautiful French omelette when we found a small typically French **café**. I was glad I spoke a little French so communicating was not too difficult. In London Vince also got plenty of walking exercise, so much so that we had to take a rest in Hyde Park.

Well, before we knew it we were at London airport saying "good-bye." Vince had a flight back to the U.S. within an hour, but I had to wait all day--not a happy time with lots of worries going through my head: my oncoming divorce that I already had put into motion before leaving for Europe, all the workload ahead of me, the loneliness living by myself in the small apartment and, of course, Vince being so far away! I was glad when I could finally get on the plane and for the next 20 hours, I didn't have any responsibilities and whatever worries I had, there was absolutely nothing I could do about it right now. So it seemed a good idea to try and get some sleep and think of the happy times I left behind . . ..

Chapter XXXIV

After my return, I worked around the clock to satisfy my clients. It's nice when you have reached the top and you are in demand, but that also brings about a lot of responsibilities. For instance, once your designs are approved, the dress patterns are made and handed over to the workrooms to produce the sample garments, there is still a lot more work involved. It is a race against time until the whole collection can be shown to the buyers. The Designer has to be almost clairvoyant to foresee how many garments of a style will be sold, so the fabrics and accessories (like buttons) could be ordered ahead of time to be on hand when production starts. Department store buyers would not be amused if their orders didn't arrive at the specified time. In case delivery is late, you can forget to ever receive another order from them!

To avoid the hassle to preorder fabric, it was decided to design a small range of "After Five" dresses in a fabric that was always in stock (being available) from our supplier. When I placed my order for production of the garments sold, I was told that, due to an environmental problem with the dye-works in Vietnam, there was a fabric shortage and my order could not be filled! Probably the dye had gotten into their rivers and the dye-works were closed by the government. After getting over the initial shock, I spent the next days on the phone trying to contact other fabric suppliers and manufacturers in the hope that they might have some surplus fabric.

I finally managed to secure enough fabric to produce the garments on order, but most of it had to be flown in. This was a loss that had not been incorporated in the garment price, but at least we could deliver the dresses at the right time and thus keep the buyers happy.

My apartment was on the outskirts of Melbourne, so I took the train to get to work in the city. One morning I noticed two grown cats with a gorgeous black kitten on the railway grounds. Irresponsible people probably had dumped them at the railway station. That really started to worry me in case they were hungry and something would happen to them. I knew two ladies that were also cat lovers like me. They told me they would try to trap them, but it would take time as they were obviously wild cats. In the meantime, I should try and get some food to them. I spoke to the railway officials, but they made it clear that nobody would be allowed to cross the tracks. The only way to get some food to them seemed to be throwing it in a brown paper bag across the tracks when nobody was looking. I fell in love with that little black kitten. I assumed it was a girl because it moved as gracefully as a young Egyptian queen, so in my mind I gave it the name of "Cleopatra"- Cleo for short. But the cats were not my only worry! Although Vince did occasionally call, I missed the closeness and warmth in our conversation that we had shared. After such a call, I usually felt disappointed and more depressed. The only good thing to cheer me up was that most of my friends stayed in touch with me-- especially one girl that Toni also knew. But although I appreciated her calling me, she also upset me by telling me that Toni was no longer drinking and that he missed me terribly. She was sworn to secrecy regarding my phone number and whereabouts, but never failed to tell me "how unhappy he was!"

Well, I was far from being happy myself coming home from work to my small and empty apartment. I can't say that I missed Toni after all that happened in the past, but I certainly missed my home and former lifestyle. By now he must have received the divorce papers from my lawyer, and I was not surprised when he asked through my girlfriend if I would meet him at the house for a discussion. I had to think hard what to do about my situation.

With Vince's lack of emotional support, I felt all alone in the world. I still would have to wait at least a year before reaching retirement age, so I could apply for a small pension through Social Security. I also thought about that dear little kitten. I could never be so cruel as to bring it to my apartment after it had known freedom. With all this going through my mind, I agreed to meet Toni at the house. To my surprise, he was almost the charming Toni of long ago--and there wasn't a drink in the house! He promised that nothing like in the past was ever going to happen again and pleaded for me to cancel divorce proceedings. Like a fool, I fell for his promises again! He offered to drive me "home," but I said "no thanks, I'll take the train!"

Next morning at my studio, I had to call Vince and tell him of my decision. He said he had almost expected it, but asked to let him know how it was working out. I felt happy to go back to my home but uneasy at the same time because I knew Toni too well to believe his promises would really last!

I couldn't help thinking that Vince sounded almost relieved that once again he could avoid making a decision. His wife-God bless her-must have really been the driving force in their marriage . . .!

Chapter XXXV

After a week of reorganizing my work schedule, canceling my apartment (thank goodness I hadn't taken out a lease!) and, last not least, meeting with my lawyer, I returned home. The nice female lawyer was quite worried about my decision to return to Toni and warned me that in her view, I was making a big mistake. I explained to her my circumstances, and that my only salvation to get away would be to leave the country. In my heart, I knew in case my return to Toni was a mistake, my last resort would eventually have to be this way. But I was willing to give this reunion a last chance.

Toni seemed happy that he no longer had to cater for himself. He was not drinking, but still chain-smoking, which was not very pleasant either. The work stress and racing home to cook a meal in the evening took its toll, and my heart started to react again with occasional arrhythmia attacks. Because of all the terrible domestic violence issues caused by Toni, I had started to sleep in the front room. Unfortunately, it didn't have a door. After my return I continued to sleep by myself because I didn't know whether the "peace" was really going to last. I'm sure Toni wasn't too pleased, but I thought he should prove that he meant what he had promised before becoming "husband and wife" again.

On my way to work, I noticed only little Cleo without her parents! A phone call to my cat ladies explained why! They had been able to trap the parents, but Cleo was too quick to get out of the cage before the trap door came down. Now I really had worries! Thank goodness Cleo had become used to me throwing food across to the other side, so she still waited every day at the same spot. My friends said the time to trap Cleo would be in the evening with me also being there because she knows me. But how could I get away from home in the evening without Toni being suspicious? He had told me once before he did not want any more pets! My chance came when Toni decided to fly to Sydney for a master painters' convention. I quickly informed my two cat friends and we met in the evening that same day. I hadn't been allowed to feed Cleo on my way home from work and couldn't bear to see her disappointment. But this way we hoped that she would be really hungry and eat the food inside the cage and not run out before the trap door could close. Although we were not allowed to cross the tracks, we found out that we could enter from the other side on the esplanade that ran along the river Yarra parallel to the tracks.

It was one of those early spring evenings filled with sheer magic. All the lanterns on the esplanade were lit and a river boat was slowly cruising down the Yarra. We carefully set the trap and huddled together on a nearby bench holding our breath. Soon a little "hungry" shadow was busily moving around checking out the unfamiliar cage. We were euphoric when we heard the trap door shut with Cleo still inside!

I was hoping that Toni would be in a good mood after his return so I could coax him into letting me keep Cleo. But my friends warned me that Cleo was a wild cat and not used to close contact with humans. It would take time and patience to tame her. I was to keep her in a cage and only take her out on a leash so she could get used to her new environment. When Toni arrived back home, he wasn't too pleased, but I said I rescued Cleo from being "run over" so he accepted my story.

Unfortunately, though, he had started drinking again. I didn't dare to say anything, but I had this terrible feeling of "déjà vu" . . . .

Chapter XXXVI

I wasn't far wrong in my presentiment regarding Toni's return to drinking. Now that he thought I wouldn't make another attempt to leave him, he took full advantage of that, and soon I was in the same predicament as before. He also knew that I would not leave Cleo, who didn't want to be near him and who was very much my cat. It really had not taken me long to get her used to her new life. I had started to take her out of her cage on a lead for a while, until one day I set her free in the garden. To my horror, she jumped over the neighbor's fence but returned immediately, so I knew that she was happy to stay with me.

Whenever Toni started ranting and raving and--so far--only verbally abusing me, she went into hiding, but always returned to sleep with me when things were quiet again!

I realized that the lady-lawyer had been right in her prediction. I could see that it would only be a matter of time until I would have to make a decision. Because Toni could never admit to being an alcoholic, I even started to attend AA meetings in the hope to find out from other people in similar circumstances how to deal with or help Toni with his alcohol abuse! But, after a few meetings I was no wiser and even more depressed.

All of our friends were aware of the situation, but because they had known Toni in better times, they were equally sympathetic toward him. I still had a lot of work, whereas Toni's clients had almost all disappeared. So he only worked very sporadically and I never knew whether he would be home or at work. I guess being forced to keep my clients happy by working nonstop was my salvation in keeping my sanity.

Apart from working at my studio, I also had two clients who sometimes required me on their premises. There I had to act happy and bright and nobody ever suspected how miserable my home situation was. Of course, when Toni wasn't working, it was an open door to either line up some drinking buddies or spend the day drinking by himself.

Sometimes I felt almost sorry for him because he was once a handsome, talented and good-hearted man! Coming home in the evening to cook a meal, not knowing what mood he'd be in had become a nightmare that I had to live with, with yet no escape route in sight!

Gradually the situation went from bad to worse. As it happened before, he started to become violent--throwing things around, demolishing furniture and, worst of all, laying his hands on me. If I wanted to avoid injury, I had to run for my life and sneak back into the house when I could be sure he'd be asleep. Because I hadn't been able to eat the meal I had cooked with him throwing the plates off the table, I started to store energy drinks under my bed to keep up my strength. The police did not want any part of it, told me to stay with friends, or there were places where women threatened by domestic violence could find shelter. How could I leave Cleo and cope with my workload going to a shelter!? I had to face reality and make a decision before it would be too late!

Chapter XXXVII

I felt it was time to tell my family that I was thinking about leaving Toni for good and come home. Sigrid and Carla had known all along that it would eventually come to that. I owned a third of my parent's property, so at least I would have a place to stay. Vince, who had called at my studio from time to time, was horrified when I told him what was going on. Once he even asked "Did I want to come to the U.S," but when I almost accepted his offer, he kind of backed off again by saying "Do you think this will work?" I thought to myself "yes, that's my Cancerian--one step forward and two back!" No, that wasn't the solution!

My main concern was Cleo; no way would I desert her and leave her behind!! If I booked a flight with an airline, I wanted a direct flight to Vienna (Austria) with Cleo being on the same plane. Fortunately, I found out that there was an Austrian airline that provided direct flights, except for a short touchdown in Bangkok. Well, that would save Cleo the trauma changing flights at Heathrow Airport in London. But, what would I live on back in Austria without income? Fortunately, I was now at retirement age and therefore eligible for a small pension. I personally applied at Social Security so that I could let them know of my situation, and that all correspondence must only be directed to my studio! No way must Toni find out about my plans!

When they heard my sad story--especially when I broke down and cried--they were very sympathetic. They even took me into a small room so I could calm down, and also made me a cup of tea. Yes, the Australian people will always have a special place in my heart!

Having taken care of this important matter, it was time to contact the airline. The problem was that I really didn't know when I would be able to leave. Toni would have sooner "taken me out" of my existence than letting me go. It's like when a dog no longer wants his bone, but he'd bury it rather than letting another dog have it! So I knew I could only escape if Toni wasn't there.

I had an idea that he had a job prospect but I couldn't be sure when he would start work. Also, I still had so much to do, so I really only wanted to make inquiries and talk to a booking clerk regarding Cleo's transport.

I was lucky to talk to a nice guy who gave me the phone number of a company specializing in pet-transport in connection with their airline. When I called, I also talked to a sympathetic man. He advised me, after listening to my predicament, to arrange with a friend to take in Cleo a day before leaving, and he would pick her up from there in a special travel cage and bring her to the airport for me to check her in on my flight. I knew instantly that for this I could count on my cat- friend who helped to trap Cleo from the railway station that memorable evening.

With all these phone calls and inquiries, it's a wonder I still got any work done! I told only one of my closest friends about my plans. She assured me she would help me all the way, even if she needed to get out of bed in the middle of the night, if I was desperate for a driver. God Bless her--that is a true friend! My other friends who had the workroom next to my studio also knew, but they disapproved of Toni for a long time and had no contact with him anyway. Sometimes, when I was on my own, I started to walk around in the house looking at all the lovely pieces I had bought and collected. I asked myself what I could live without, or what had such sentimental value for me that I couldn't bear to leave it behind.

I also ordered a big wooden travel box from a shipping company to be delivered to my studio and slowly started to remove items from the house without Toni noticing. With his drinking so far gone, he no longer was the alert and observant Toni of long ago. He had incredible mood changes--one minute nice and the next minute mean and abusive. Sometimes, when he was very drunk, he would boast about his successes with women and let slip out a lot about his overnight stays with his "childhood girlfriend" when we were in Austria after his cousin was killed in a road accident. I had long suspected that anyway. Even when we were in company, he continued to act as if he still was the irresistible Toni of his youth. In those moments, I felt embarrassed and almost sorry for him, and could not believe that I had ever been in love with this man!!!

Chapter XXXVIII

The guy from the pet-transport company called and informed me that Cleo would require an import license for Austria that should be sent here, which would then be attached to her travel cage. Also she must be vaccinated against rabies before leaving. After that, she would have to enter Austria within 30 days. Because Australia never had a case of rabies, veterinarians did not have any vaccine. I would have to bring Cleo to the quarantine station near the airport. What a problem!

How could I get her out of the house with Toni being at home?! I prayed for an opportunity at the right time. Worse, a call to the quarantine station informed me that I would have to arrive with her before noon!

One morning when I was about to leave for work, Toni--fairly sober—announced that he had a job inquiry and would drive there to give an estimate for a painting job. After he left, I quickly rang my driver-friend who came straight away and picked up Cleo and me. Poor Cleo was not very pleased when I put her into the cage. It was already mid-morning, and it was a fairly long drive to the quarantine station. It wasn't easy to find and we got a bit panicky when we got hopelessly lost. But--fortunately, we made it in the nick of time as the officer there was just getting ready to leave.

Cleo, who by now probably doubted my loyalty to her, got her shot and we were anxiously racing home. I hoped Toni would not be there as yet, before he would get suspicious. My friend stopped at the car park at the train station opposite the street where I lived. I told her to keep the cage and I put Cleo in my roomy bag that I always took to work carrying dresses or dress patterns.

What must Cleo have been thinking?! Crossing the street, I saw Toni's van was already parked in our driveway. I had to quickly think of a story why I had returned from work. I shoved darling Cleo into the house mumbling "she had been out on the driveway again." and "that I had to come home from work because I felt sick." Toni, watching TV with a drink in front of him, "bought" the story. To make it more plausible, I even went to bed for a short while. I couldn't afford to really be sick; I had too much work!

Asking Toni if he got the painting job, the good news was that he said "yes, he did!" Would that provide me with an opportunity toward my escape?? The bad news was that Cleo got very sick over the next few days. I even had to take her to the vet, but thank goodness she got over it. The quarantine officer—not being used to rabies in the country--probably gave her a bigger dose than she should have had.

My next move was to see my lawyers, make a will, file for divorce again, and discuss what would have to be done with our joint ownership of property. Unfortunately, real estate was down but nevertheless the house would have to be auctioned after my departure and a lawyer would act on my behalf. Toni was not to be handed the divorce papers until I was safely out of the country. I tried not to think too much and hoped somebody "above" would guide me out of this nightmare.

Would I ever be leading a normal happy life?? I thought of the saying: "What doesn't kill you makes you stronger" and hoped that it would ring true for me!

Chapter XXXIX

Carla, who I had asked to obtain the import license for Cleo, informed me that according to her inquiries, no import license was necessary. The guy from the pet transport agency found that hard to believe, but accepted it. In the hope of Toni starting work shortly, I booked my and Cleo's flight for 2 weeks ahead. Surely, Toni would be working by then?! But I should have known him better! I had to cancel! After the third time, the nice booking clerk said (by now we were on a first-name basis): "Melanie, I can cancel you out, but I don't know if I can reserve the window seat you want next time you book again." How patient he was, but perhaps he felt an obligation to help a fellow Austrian who was in trouble! He even connected me to a ground stewardess who promised to help me with checking in my luggage at the airport. I had explained to her that I was leaving my aggressive husband and would have some valuable heirloom pieces in my suitcases.

By now, I was a bundle of nerves and started to move like a sleepwalker. Perhaps the one from "above" couldn't stand the suspense any longer either. I wondered if I came close to a breaking point because right now I was "down in the dumps." This afternoon, I tried to concentrate on my work at the studio when Toni called in the afternoon and asked very nicely "if I could come home a bit earlier, pick up some food and a bottle of champagne on the way so I wouldn't have to cook!" I should have been suspicious because he hardly ever called. Also, had he run out of his usual supply of wine because he wanted me to bring a bottle of champagne? I was tired, and if for a change he wanted to be nice, I wasn't going to object! After my arrival at home, Toni was already sitting at the table waiting for me. He expertly opened the champagne and, still being nice, asked me to sit down and have a drink with him. One glass was alright on an empty stomach, but when he poured me another glass, I started to get nervous. I wanted to get him to eat something, and I was hungry myself. No, he didn't want to eat! "Why can't I ever sit with him and talk!!!"

My alarm bells rang and I could see things were getting out of hand again! So I got up, carved the roast chicken and arranged it with the salad on the plates. Well, it made him so mad that he swiped the plates off the table and--once again--I had to run for my life! Fortunately, I had learned to always leave my pocketbook near the entrance door with some money and the house key. The police, as many times before, advised me to stay with a friend overnight. I knew "this was it;" I had reached the stage of "no return!"

I called one of my friends that worked next to my studio; she told me to get a taxi and come straight to where she lived. From there, I called my driver-friend and the cat-lady to be on call in the morning.

After a sleepless night I went to the police station again at 6 a.m. and asked "would somebody accompany me to the house to pick up my cat." They looked at me as if I was crazy being more concerned about my cat than my own safety! Anyway, they would not be able to help me until the new shift arrived at 8 a.m. Well, that left me no choice; I had to get Cleo before Toni woke up! I had called my driver-friend from the police station, asked her to let my cat-lady friend know we would bring Cleo, and asked her to wait for me at the car park with the cage.

Thank goodness the house was quiet when I sneaked inside. I was praying that I could find Cleo and that Toni had not let her out into the garden like he sometimes did out of spite. He knew I wanted her safely inside during the night. Luckily, I found Cleo hiding on a chair under the table, so I grabbed her and quickly left as quietly as I could. The poor darling was in shock, trembling with fright and cold. It was a miserable chilly and rainy morning with the approach of the Australian winter. Fortunately, she was wearing a collar with her name tag that I could grab and hold onto.

Waiting for my friend at the car park felt like an eternity when it really wasn't very long at all. I was glad to put Cleo into the secure cage because I had been so afraid she would break loose of my grip being so frightened. We didn't have far to drive to deliver Cleo to her temporary "asylum" until she and I would be reunited at the airport.

The police weren't overjoyed when I turned up again--especially when I confirmed that Toni had a gun! When the new shift arrived, two policemen reluctantly agreed to accompany me to the house. Toni was already on the phone trying to call friends to find out where I had stayed overnight. I thought to myself how right I had been to collect Cleo so early! I'm sure any later and it would have been catastrophic! One of the policemen was occupying Toni in a conversation, while the other one was watching me gathering some of my belongings. Most important were my passport and documents, and then I spread a blanket on the floor and went about the house and collected what, in my mind, I already had decided to take into my "new life." My policeman must have had bad nerves because he kept telling me "hurry up, aren't you finished yet ----" Well, when I was, I asked him to call me a taxi and watch that Toni would not follow me! But I needn't have worried about that. Knowing Toni he would be on the phone calling people and drowning his anger in alcohol!

Before I finally left the house, I turned around and took one last look, like I had seen me do so often in a dream.

When I arrived at the building where I had my studio, my friend where I had stayed overnight was already waiting for me and helped me carry the blanket with my belongings into the elavator to my studio on the 7th floor.

I couldn't believe that my nightmare was so close to ending! I had reached the "river of no return."

Chapter XL

I n my studio, I felt like I was "out of my body standing beside myself." I made a lot of phone calls and even tried to concentrate on my work. My friends next door ordered lunch for me which I badly needed. At last, the long day ended and it was strange, but nice, to travel home with my friend to spend another night there. Although I was in a traumatic situation, we actually were almost in a "party mood!" I felt as if I was coming out of a bad sickness and had entered the recovery stage. I was so exhausted that I slept like a baby!

The next day was spent finalizing many things and booking our flight for the fourth time (Yes, I got my window seat!). When I assured my booking-friend that "this was it," he must have said "hallelujah" to himself!! I finished packing the box with the rescued items from the house and the shipping agent came straight away, sealed it and took it away. I had to cancel my studio, pay all my bills, called all my clients-- who were very upset--and informed Carla when I would arrive in Vienna. I also had to see my accountant regarding paying my taxes.

When I called Vince, he seemed to be very relieved to hear the news. He said he had been worried about my safety and I promised to keep in touch once I was back in Austria. I had some worrying calls from Toni on my voice mail, either pleading for me to come back or threatening to kill me when he sounded very drunk. Sad as it was to leave Australia after 38 years, I could hardly wait to be on the plane.

Waiting for Cleo to be delivered to me at the airport nearly cost me my last nerves. It was almost the end of check-in time for her when the pet-transport guy finally arrived. His car had broken down and he had to wait for another vehicle. Poor Cleo cried when she saw me, but I was glad that they had provided her with a big and roomy travel cage that had a safety lock. It nearly broke my heart when I checked her in and had to let her go again. Well, there was nothing I could do!

My friends that came with me to the airport were a real comfort to me, and I'll always be grateful to them!

At the luggage check-in, I was met by the nice stewardess who had kept her word and helped me to check my suitcases through the security procedures. My God, today I would have been arrested as a terrorist because the X-ray machine showed all sorts of knives (my family silver) and suspicious looking "instruments" like my beautiful antique servers. When the guy at the X-ray exclaimed "What is this?" She told him to "just check it through." She even personally led me to my window seat and promised to look in on Cleo and assured me that they had heated the area where she would stay during the flight.

I could not believe when "takeoff" finally happened, and a new chapter of my life had begun. I hoped that Cleo would survive the trauma and that we both would be happy in a more peaceful life!!

Chapter XLI

I don't remember much about the long 21-hour flight; I was either worrying about Cleo or dozing in a semi-conscious state grateful to be away from all the trauma of the last few days. When we touched down in Bangkok, I wished that I could see how Cleo was doing! What a relief it was when my stewardess friend came to tell me that Cleo was doing fine! She had been sitting up fully alert, probably hoping that I would come and take her out of her "confinement." Just to know that she was coping made me feel better!

At last we came close to our destination, circling over the outskirts of Vienna, so I got really excited! After landing, I expected to have no trouble in collecting Cleo, but none of the officials knew anything about a cat! I raced from one to the other; one heartless person even remarked that "probably she had been left in a container when they unloaded some of the cargo in Bangkok!"

With Cleo missing, I was close to a nervous breakdown! Nearly everybody had left by now, but one of the customer service windows was still open with two officers in attendance. They didn't know anything about a cat either. I told them if they didn't find out what had happened to my cat, I would scream so loud that the whole population of Vienna would hear it!

They could see I meant it, so one officer made a hurried phone call: "Your cat is at cargo in a building not far from here!" That was like music to my ears!

I ran outside. Carla, who didn't know why I had been delayed, thought I had lost my mind when I jumped into a taxi yelling "I have to find Cleo!" The taxi driver was a nice young man and, thank God, not an old grouchy one. I told him to take me to "cargo." "Where is that?," he inquired. I was so upset that I barked at him: "You should know; I come from Australia and don't live here!"

When he heard of my missing cat, he assured me we would find it, and after driving a while, we came to a big building that looked like what we were after. On the ground floor were a lot of big boxes stacked up, and the man working there said that nearly all the offices were closed because it was the first of May. That is a big day in Austria, similar to Labor Day in the U.S.

Well, we climbed from floor to floor, all offices were closed until we found one still open. When we dashed in with our inquiry "Have you got a black cat?", the attendant said "Yes, we have." But they would not release her because she had no import license! So Carla, who was supposed to send me the license to Australia, had goofed!! Nearly in tears, I asked what I could do, so the kind attendant said I could buy the license for 350 Austrian shillings (Austria had not yet been converted to Euros.). But I only had Australian money that they would not accept! I asked my young driver if he had 350 shillings? After fishing around in his pockets, he produced the money, we collected Cleo who cried--I hoped with joy--and drove back to where I had last seen Carla. But she was gone!! So I thought it would be best to drive home. I remarked to my nice driver that this probably had been the first time that he had to pay for a passenger! He agreed with a chuckle and said it had provided him with a good story to tell his mates!

When we arrived at home, Carla, much relieved but still puzzled what had happened, paid for my fare. I was sorry that, in the excitement, I forgot to ask the driver for a contact number in case I should need him again, and also so I could really thank him. Well, my arrival did not seem important enough why so many people were gathered at Sigrid's apartment. No, they were there for a party to celebrate Simon's (Sigrid's second husband's) retirement. I knew all the guests from long ago, but after a short while I excused myself and reclined to what used to be Mama's apartment, but which now was to be my new "home." Cleo was glad to be out of her cage; I put food and water there for her and I guess we were both too exhausted to take notice of our new surroundings . . .

Chapter XLII

Next morning, I took a critical look and came to the conclusion that the apartment was going to need a complete "makeover" to be comfortable. Mama always thought of the family's needs first, and that's why it was in such a deplorable state. And—what had happened to the only big room that also was part of Mama's apartment?? Yes, you guessed it--Sigrid had "included" it into her third of our inheritance. I didn't want to start animosity so I kept quiet. I had to be content with the two small rooms and a part that once had been a passage, which I would have to convert into a kitchen and bathroom. Well, right now I could do nothing. I had to wait for my divorce and the auction sale of the house to get any money. At five one morning, my lawyer called from the auction and said "There was only one bid!" Real estate was at its lowest and the money offered was probably a third of its value. When I cried in shock, the lawyer advised me to accept the offer. If I allowed Toni to stay there, he would let it run down and decrease the value even more. I swallowed hard and took my lawyer's advice and accepted. I can imagine how Toni cursed me!

It was now June and the weather was very pleasant. Cleo enjoyed the park like surroundings of our garden, and she even had a nice cat boyfriend who visited her every day. Any other cat intruders were chased away by the two!

Carla was very supportive; she lived by herself and was glad to have my company. Her son Karl was studying law and lived away from home. Sigrid didn't have much time and often gave piano lessons to young people.

Her son André had set up a small café with an adjoining art gallery in Germany, thanks to what was left from the inheritance that his father Nicholas had provided. He had attended the Academy of Fine Arts for a few years, and Sigrid hoped that he would succeed in gaining the international fame that she had failed to achieve as a pianist.

André certainly acted as he already was a celebrity, but his present achievements were in no relation to his spending. He was forever in debt, and Sigrid's husband Simon was obliged to cover his luxuries thanks to his fabulous pension. Simon was a gentle, kindhearted man, liked by all but completely under Sigrid's domination.

Neither Carla nor Sigrid was very interested to hear about my traumatic times in Australia, so I kept them to myself. Sometimes I felt like an intruder who was disrupting their lifestyles by claiming what rightly belonged to me. It was obvious that my apartment had been used by Sigrid as a storage facility for some of André's belongings.

I was almost sure there was going to be trouble when the renovation of my apartment would start in spring. But for now, I did not complain, especially when Vince wrote that he was coming. He was an easy-go-lucky guy and would not be concerned about the present state of my apartment. We had a few pleasant weeks, and we even took a bus trip to Prague. Sigrid had offered to take care of Cleo. I was glad that she also liked cats. This time, Vince and I could relax because there was no danger of Toni turning up. That chapter was closed!

Chapter XLIII

My divorce became final in the fall and I received the money from the auction, with legal fees taking a big chunk from what was already very little. But at least I could make plans to renovate in the spring.

The winter was not very pleasant; there was no good heating source. Thank goodness Carla loaned me a portable heater. How did Mama survive? The lovely ceramic stove did not seem to work. Mama had it converted to electricity and something was wrong with the switch.

I had no phone, although I could use Sigrid's. But I did not want to bother them. Vince wrote occasionally, but he was not an ardent letter writer so I did not know how he felt about our relationship. When he was here in the summer, he hinted once or twice about something "permanent," but I really had not thought about another marriage and, I guess, neither did he!

Petra and I had renewed our former friendship in a big way and, through her, many of my former classmates contacted me. It was nice to meet with them and it seemed a bit like old times. The only thing I missed was that I had nobody who spoke English. After 38 years in Australia, it had become second nature to me. But when spring came and I started renovating my apartment, I had no time to think about anything else. Surprisingly, Sigrid was very helpful; she seemed to enjoy planning and also went with me to buy essential items like tiles, appliances and everything necessary for renovating. She was good at measuring so that the new appliances would fit into the narrow area which once had been a passage. There certainly wasn't much room to fit a kitchen and bathroom into it. She even helped by wallpapering one room, which covered all the cracks in the walls and ceiling. It started to shape up very nicely. Sometimes to get to my bed, Cleo and I had to climb over a toilet, bathtub, washbasin, etc. that had been delivered waiting to be installed in its proper place. When finally everything was finished, I felt I had a home again.

The next winter was a lot more pleasant; I had electric heating units installed and finally got the switch of the ceramic stove working. Now I could invite my friends to dinner parties and Carla was always included. Sometimes we had family gatherings with Sigrid and Simon as well, and all seemed to be going along nicely. I was happy to be reunited with my family after so many years being away in Australia.

Chapter XLIV

S ummer had arrived again and with this also Vince, who seemed to enjoy having a summer residence in Austria! I enjoyed his visits, and because I had known him for so long we were like an old couple. But after 3 days, Vince got a call from one of his two sons. It was the sad news that his mother had passed away.

I had to race to the Tourist Bureau and book the next available flight back to the U.S. I felt very sorry for Vince; I knew what it was like to lose a parent. Waiting with him at the airport, I asked whether he would come back after this was all over? The answer was "But by then it will already be August!!" That really surprised me! Did he regard his visits to me as only being "a summer event?" It was a hard pill to swallow! Did he think I would waste my time waiting till he found it convenient to reappear? But I didn't say anything and thought maybe he didn't mean it to sound this way because he was upset over what awaited him at home. Eventually a letter arrived and our correspondence trickled on, but no plan evolved.

Spring had arrived and I got fidgety. Was he again coming this summer? I decided to find out and called him. "Vince, what do you intend to do?" Perhaps he mistook my question for "What are your intentions?", which to him may have sounded like: "Are you going to marry me?"

His answer was a real shocker! He said in typical undecided fashion that I knew so well: "I don't know what I want!" That did it!!

It was like a slap in my face. So I said as sweetly as I could, "Well, in this case I wish you all the best for the future, and perhaps one day you'll know what you want!" Vince immediately realized his mistake and he was still rattling on "how he thought the world of me . . .," but I just hung up. Yes, I cried for a couple of days, but then I consoled myself that at least I found out Vince was not the "true love" that I thought he was . . .

Chapter XLV

I couldn't believe we were writing the year 1994 and I had been back in Austria for two years! I kept myself busy renewing old friendships, enrolled in a French refresher course, joined silk painting classes I had started in Australia, and enjoyed being a family member. Cleo was the happiest she had ever been. Sometimes, she would race in from the garden and jump on my lap to let me know she was having a wonderful time. The only thing I missed was talking to somebody in English now that Vince was no longer part of my life.

One of my friends had been a member of the "White Mice traffic police force" in post WWII, who were working in conjunction with the American Military Police. My friend Willi showed me an article in a magazine about a former MP (Military Police) who wanted to visit Vienna hoping to find some of his Austrian friends. Willi had recognized him by the photo and had contacted him. "Melanie, you are bi-lingual and you could help this guy! Why don't you write to him; you have more time than I do!" was Willi's suggestion.

I thought about it for a day, but then I liked the idea of a chance to speak English again. Willi had assured me that the American was a nice guy and furthermore I presumed by his Italian name that he was probably married with half a dozen kids!! So I wrote to him and offered my help. I had already forgotten about my letter because it took a while till I got an answer. Mario had been in Florida and only received my letter when he returned to New Jersey. He sounded grateful for my offer to act as his interpreter, and I was impressed by his complete honesty about his financial situation. So we started corresponding and exchanged photos; it filled the void in missing the English language. Mario and I seemed to have a lot in common; we both liked classical music and jazz, so we already had found many things to write about. Did I discover some romantic sparks flying by some of his remarks?? I had a feeling this was not another Vince. I must admit I enjoyed this feeling to soon meet somebody who was no newcomer to attract a lady's attention! My suspicion was confirmed when Mario sent me a tape with Sinatra singing "Love is Wonderful the Second Time Around. . ." I thought: "Am I imagining things, or had Mario chosen this song to send me a message?" Well, I told myself not to imagine something that might never happen! Anyway, I didn't want any more romantic disappointments in my life!

Mario asked me if I could find him a reasonably priced room somewhere other than Vienna City because he couldn't afford to stay there; their prices were far too expensive for his budget. So Petra and I found one on a nice street in the town where we lived. The house owner always rented some rooms in summer, sometimes even to foreign students who attended the university in Vienna; an American therefore would be welcome.

The big day arrived and Willi and I met at the airport. Mario had mentioned in an earlier letter that he had received many invitations from people who offered he could stay with them, or others who wanted something. They were probably under the impression that he was a "rich American."

While waiting at the airport, Willi and I spotted a lady with presumably her husband who eyed me suspiciously when Willi had a sign with "Welcome Mario" in his hand. We giggled as we watched this lady, who obviously wanted to be the first in line to welcome Mario at the "arrival gate" so that she could bring him home as her personal "trophy!" When Mario finally came through the gate, Willi took a photo of Mario and me with the welcome sign displayed on his suitcases. He also took a photo with the lady, her husband and Mario, but to their disappointment Mario left with us! When we arrived in my town after the drive from the airport, we took Mario to his room and introduced him to his "landlady". He seemed happy with his accommodation.

At my place, I had a nice lunch prepared on the terrace with a bottle of champagne to celebrate Mario's arrival, but he shocked me when he said "Don't give me much champagne!!" Willi and I looked at each other and I thought: "What do we have here; is he a tea-totaler??" Much later when we knew each other better, Mario explained that he once got sick drinking pink champagne (which is sweet) at a party and ever since then even the word "champagne" made his stomach feel queasy. Willi offered to drive him to his room, but it was a lovely day and I promised to see that he got to his room later.

Seeing I had no success offering champagne, I asked Mario if he would like a glass of red wine? That was a better offer to an "Italian!" So we just sat and talked. He told me about his failed marriage to a woman who had only used him for her own benefits and furthermore had cheated on him. And, oh how nice it was to have a sympathetic man listen to my story! I knew wherever the road would lead us, we would always be "friends."

Time had disappeared so fast, and drinking wine reminded me that we also needed some food! I remembered I had a pizza in the freezer that I had made some days ago. I think I won Mario's "Italian" heart with the pizza that night! It was late and pitch dark when Mario left. It had also started to rain with gusty winds. However, Mario felt confident he would find the way to his room by himself and would not let me accompany him. So I loaned him my umbrella and hoped for the best. I told him I would come and pick him up for breakfast the next morning. Before falling asleep, I felt happier than I had been in a long time. I had found a new "friend!!!"

Chapter XLVI

When I arrived next morning to pick up Mario for breakfast, he was in a terrible state! He said he got disoriented walking in the dark, the umbrella blew inside out in the blustery rain, and there was a girl walking in front of him who kept turning around looking at him as if she thought that he was the "Boston strangler" who was following her. He was afraid that she might cry for help and he would be picked up by the police!

When he finally found the building and opened the gate, all the lights went on as if somebody was already waiting for him! He didn't know that the lights came on automatically for the boarders! Then, when he wanted to take a shower before going to bed, the bathroom was not locked and a young girl was just taking a shower!

Furthermore, the whole house smelled as if somebody was smoking marijuana! Poor Mario, what an ending to a nice evening! It was easy to see that he was not happy with his room!

When Willi came and heard Mario's story, we decided to move him in with me until we would find another room for him. He could sleep on the sofa in my garden room. Willi would go with Mario to see the landlady, explain that he was taking Mario on a trip to Germany, and reclaim his deposit.

Everything worked out according to plan, and Mario seemed relieved and happy! Over the next few days, he was a perfect gentleman who did not take advantage of the situation.

I introduced him to Carla and Sigrid, who seemed a bit surprised, and I also took him to meet some of my friends. Even Cleo accepted him, although she was jealous at first! Every now and then, I caught Mario looking at me as if he wouldn't mind getting to know me a little better?! It was a nice feeling, and I enjoyed it!

A friend invited us to a concert of Viennese music. She thought Mario might enjoy it, and as she was married to an American, he would welcome the opportunity to meet one of his countrymen.

We had a wonderful time and celebrated afterward with a few glasses of wine. When Mario and I arrived home, we were still talking happily about the concert and—had it been the wine? -- Mario suddenly took me in his arms, kissed me--and before I knew what and how it happened--we were a "couple!!"

Falling asleep together, we both knew that we had turned a page to enter a new and happier chapter in our lives!

Chapter XLVII

I t was wonderful to be in love again! I felt safe and secure and each day Mario and I became closer.

Even my sisters seemed happy that there was a real man in the house. Cleo also "approved" so it looked as if 1994 was going to be a good year for all of us. My friends liked Mario right from the start, and we had many get-togethers. We always included Carla as well, and I guess she really enjoyed to be invited to take part. Was Sigrid getting a bit jealous?? But she was either giving piano lessons, or she and her husband Simon were occupied doing something else.

I loved both my sisters, and to know I had a family was the only thing that kept me going in my worst time in Australia. But I sometimes also felt that I was like a buffer in the middle between the two. I think it was partly because Sigrid always seemed to make her aristocratic heritage being felt. Carla, who was from Mama's first marriage, often walked away looking hurt because of Sigrid's attitude. On the other hand, Sigrid was envious that Carla occupied the complete first floor, whereas she only had Papa's former surgery rooms (plus the big room she appropriated herself with from my inheritance!!)

There was never any real animosity on the surface, but I could sense the undercurrent in their relationship. Grandpapa, the General, certainly came through in Sigrid's genes!

More and more Mario was helping with repairs in the house; he always knew the answer to fix any problem. Carla's windows were in bad shape, some of them ready to fall out. But she only had a small pension and could not afford to engage a professional. So we decided to help her out. Even before we decided to do that, it was agreed to regard any work we did as our contribution toward the upkeep of the property in lieu of money. Neither Mario nor I had a big pension like Simon. Of course, we paid for our own expenses, and whenever I could afford it, I also paid into the "house fund."

So we started the first-story project and even refused invitations from friends because it was essential to take advantage of good weather.

I think that's when Sigrid got really jealous! Carla wanted her window panes painted white, but Sigrid objected because hers were green and she didn't want to change!! She also felt that Mario should at least do something for her by painting her entrance door. But, as with Carla's windows, it was not only the painting but scraping off layers of the old paint. And after having done that for all the 14 windows upstairs, I flatly refused to confront Mario with another project. I thought they could well afford to pay a professional painter. My refusal didn't go down well with Sigrid, but seeing she and Simon left for their vacation, I hoped that a happier atmosphere would prevail after their return.

To celebrate the completion of Carla's windows, we had a wonderful party with our friends. I designed a big medal declaring Mario "window man of the year," Carla made a speech and our friends applauded as we decorated Mario with his award. It was the crowning glory of a lot of hard work, although Mario looked a bit embarrassed. Nevertheless, I thought he enjoyed his big moment!

Chapter XLVIII

Mario loved our apartment; although small, it contained everything we needed. In summer, it was lovely in the morning to sit on our terrace and look out into the garden. Cleo and "her boyfriend," who came to visit her every morning, were happily playing in the front yard where we could watch them. At night, I always kept Cleo inside; I wanted her to be safe because there were still wild nocturnal animals on the ground..

All in all it was a pleasant life with Mario going back to the U.S. when his visa had expired and coming back as soon as possible. I think he loved Austria even more than I did. Every time Mario returned, we had a big celebration with family and friends. Sometimes I sensed that Sigrid was a bit jealous of me being so happy with Mario. She could be very hurtful at times. Simon was a gentle and kind man who comforted me whenever that happened. I think he must have suffered under her domineering attitude. Sigrid even admitted to me that, although she appreciated Simon's big pension (which mainly went to André supporting his extravagant lifestyle!), she didn't feel like showering him with love!!! I became very concerned when she told me that André was thinking of coming back to Vienna. Even without telling me, I knew the reason for it. Whatever he ventured into had to be done in "grand style." So he had opened a café and adjoining gallery in a small rural town in Bavaria, Germany. I once saw these premises on a visit with Sigrid and could not imagine it would ever be successful in that location. The country folks there were only interested to have a few drinks, a snack and chatting with some of their "buddies"--none of this high class stuff that André wanted to introduce them to. I believe he had even ordered lobster for the menu!! Of course, it turned out to be another financial failure.

But my real concern was that his marriage was on rocky ground and he wanted a divorce. His second wife was a pretty girl he had met in a bar where she was working as a barmaid. I liked her; she was uncomplicated and good natured, but André completely overshadowed her. I was shocked when Sigrid said that he had at last (?) found the perfect woman for him and had moved her in while his wife was still there!! I couldn't help but tell Sigrid that I didn't approve of the way André went about ending his marriage! But, of course, whatever gave André pleasure was alright with Sigrid. I was beginning to worry what the future would bring!

Apart from these new developments, Mario and I couldn't have been happier. Every now and then, Mario would bring up the subject of getting married. Although I never thought I would marry again, it was exciting to think about it. We could live partly in Austria and the U.S. and enjoy the best of two continents. It would be nice to get married in Vienna among family and friends. We could then have a short "honeymoon" in the U.S. where Mario would introduce me to his relatives and friends. Well, it sounded like a good idea, but it would involve a lot of legal procedures. All Mario's and even some of my documents would have to go to a notarized interpreter's office which would be very costly. In the U.S. none of this would be necessary because my Australian documents were already in English. That seemed to be the obvious solution.

So we broke the news to my family, but it was not as joyfully received as I had hoped. I only planned to be away for 3 weeks; to her credit, Sigrid promised to take care of Cleo for that time.

Carla gave a farewell party for us and some of our closest friends, but she did not look very happy. This was a severe damper to my own happiness! I hoped that it was only because she was disappointed that we wanted to get married in the U.S. and not among the family. None of them understood the financial reason why, unfortunately, we had to do it this way.

When we were on the plane, I tried to forget about it. After all, I was on the way to **becoming a "new bride". . . .**

Chapter XLIX

My excitement mounted as our plane landed in Philadelphia. Mario had explained to me that we would be separated going through the immigration procedures. Being an American, Mario would only have to show his passport, whereas I was a visitor and would have to explain the purpose and intended length of my visit and get my passport stamped like a visa. The officer at the desk was very friendly and even wished me a happy stay. When Mario and I were reunited, we had to wait for two of his friends who would drive us to his sister's home where we would be staying.

Ever since I became introduced to American movies, the music and singing stars like Bing Crosby, Frank Sinatra and Rosemary Clooney, I sort of had a fantasy picture about the American way of life. Now I was going to find out how it was in reality.

Mario's friends made me feel very welcome and even gave me a little sightseeing tour in Philadelphia on the way to Mario's sister. I thought to myself: "I can't believe I am really here in the USA! I was amazed to see so many American flags displayed on people's properties, which made me think they really must love their country and be true patriots. Mario had told me he had lived at his sister's house ever since his divorce. So when we arrived there, my heart went out to his sister because she had been kind to him when he most needed it!

The next days were filled with activities, meeting friends, and applying for the marriage license. We were going to have a civil ceremony at the municipal building. Mario took me to a jeweler in Philadelphia where I could choose a design for my wedding ring which would be specially made. What a fascinating city where very few streets have names but mostly numbers! The harbor on the Delaware River was also impressive with big vessels like the "Moshulu" and the "United States" being moored there. I felt as if I was living in a dream!

Shopping with Mario in the big supermarkets made me feel like a kid learning to walk. We have had them in Australia too, but these were really big! I discovered that my "husband to be" had some more hidden talents. He could even cook! He told me he and a friend once had a catering business. I was very grateful that he was going to be the "chef" while staying at his sister's house. Then the "big day" finally arrived! It was a simple and touching ceremony with friends and Mario's sister and husband witnessing it.

When Mario looked into my eyes saying our marriage vows "for better or worse," I knew he meant it. His eyes were full of love and I felt I had at last found what I had longed for all my life. Our wedding night was something any girl could only dream about. Although we had been together before, this was different! It was a giving and receiving like the confirmation of the earlier given promise "to always be there for each other."

There was so much love--and the Angels were jubilant . . . .

Chapter L

The next few days were a whirlwind of invitations to celebrate our wedding. Mario's best friends, Louis, his wife Fran, and their daughter Joanne and husband Michael, gave us a wedding brunch at a restaurant in a lovely garden setting that even had a fountain.

The minute I met this family I felt as if I had always known them. It warmed my heart that their friendship with Mario seemed to immediately extend toward me. Joanne had known Mario since she and her sister were kids, so it was easy to see why, especially Joanne, was so fond of Mario. I liked this girl straight away; she was a spirited warm-hearted young lady with just a bit of tomboy in her. It was a warm and sunny day, so when we went outside in the garden to take some photos, we discovered a decorated "wedding-arch," probably in expectation for another wedding party. Joanne quickly decided to take advantage of it and positioned Mario and me under the arch for a photo. "You'll need some flowers," Joanne exclaimed, and before I realized what she was doing, she dismantled some of the flower decorations on the arch. I had trouble not to burst out laughing and spoil the photo, but Joanne's adventurous action had been unforgettable and remained another sweet memory. And, yes, she did attach the flowers back on the arch after the photo!

As if that lovely brunch had not already been enough, this generous family also took us to Atlantic City in a glamorous limousine. The boardwalk was buzzing with activity of people enjoying themselves. We dined in one of the casinos on the famous boardwalk, and I almost felt as if I was part of the "jet set." It was like a "crash course" of all the good things life can offer!

Mario's other friends treated us to dinner as well, and it was nice to get to know them all. I could see that they were all very fond of Mario, and it almost made me feel guilty for taking him away from them so soon.

Because Cleo and I had never been separated before and the 3 weeks that Sigrid had promised to take care of her were nearly up, I talked Mario into staying in the U.S. a bit longer and enjoy the company of his friends. After all, I was used to flying by myself and I now had my own phone connection in Austria so we could call each other. Mario was a bit hesitant to let me return to Vienna by myself, but after some persuasion he accepted my offer. It wasn't long before he drove me to Philadelphia airport and we hugged and kissed "good bye." I was grateful that it was a direct flight and I spent the few hours reminiscing of all the happy events that I had shared with my "new husband."

Petra and our friend picked me up at the airport; I had so much to tell them, so I was home in no time. I couldn't wait to see Cleo and tell my sisters all my exciting news! I could hear piano playing in Sigrid's apartment so I assumed she was giving a piano lesson and I would have to wait to see her. I rushed upstairs to hug Carla, but she pushed me away saying "She was expecting friends for a game of 'Bridge' and would see me in the evening." Her attitude sure was a damper on my happiness!!

Chapter LI

W as that the welcome of a sister that I truly loved? I was so upset that I thought Carla might as well have emptied a bucket of water over my head. I was nearly in tears and couldn't figure out why Carla had treated me so coldly. Was she still mad because we didn't get married in Austria?? But I thought I had explained the financial reasons behind that!!

Downhearted I went into the garden to look for Cleo. I spotted her jumping over the fence back into our yard. She looked sad and forlorn. All of a sudden she saw me; perhaps she thought she was seeing a ghost because she ran away from me! But when I called her, she turned around and ran toward me. I picked her up in my arms and held her little body close, which was comforting. I carried her back into our apartment and she rubbed against my legs as if she never wanted to leave me. The feeling was mutual and I promised that we would never be separated again! Well, meeting Carla in the evening was not much better either! She said, "Why couldn't things stay the way they were?", meaning Mario just being my boyfriend and not my husband! That figured!

Sigrid, the instigator, had alerted Carla to the fact that, due to my often occurring heart problems, Mario, and not my sister's sons, would now be the heir of my inheritance in case of my demise! So "greed" had raised its ugly head!! I could not believe how Carla had changed!

She also said I had no right to criticize André and the way he got rid of his second wife by starting an affair with another woman--I would just have to accept it! With this, I got up, thanked her and said "that I didn't have to accept anything if it was against my code of ethics!" She was so mad that she slammed the door after me and locked it! Although I was tired, sleep did not come easily! I kept waking up worrying about our future!

Mario called me early the next morning and I didn't want to burden him with my sad experience. But although I tried to hide the hurt in my voice, he sensed that something was wrong. When I confessed to him what had happened, he wanted to come straight away! But I urged him to stay on for the time we had agreed upon! However, it wasn't long before I was driving to the airport again to pick him up, only this time was very different from all the joyous occasions in the past. I feared that we were going to be very isolated!

Chapter LII

Mario's presence lifted my depression somewhat, but I still had a dim outlook on our immediate future. I suspected André's reappearance wasn't far away judging by all the clutter of items stacked up in the corridor in front of Sigrid's apartment. The confrontation with Carla had brought on another of my arrhythmia attacks, so all I could do was to rest for 2 days until I felt better.

One afternoon-Mario was watching TV-he called my attention to Sigrid and another guy measuring and taking notes right in front of our apartment. So I went outside and asked very politely "what was going on?" Sigrid said they were going to put up a fence for André's two big dogs. I objected by saying "Sigrid, put up that fence in front of your apartment and not mine!" One word led to another and what she called me was so hurtful that I could never forget it if I lived to be a "hundred." Her final statement was "that I had nothing to say in this matter!!" I was shocked, but I tried to control myself and just said, "If she insisted on a fence in front of our apartment, she would regret it one day!" I went back inside and Sigrid and her helper left "the stage" in a huff.

Mario shook his head in disbelief when I told him what had happened. That was the first time we had to take stock of our options. Mario was concerned how it would affect my impaired health if conflict was going to be the order of the day! He suggested that we might have to live in the U.S. I was too upset to think that far ahead; my thoughts were racing away without me seeing a way out!

To my surprise, work erecting the fence did start in front of Sigrid's apartment. I was glad of that because at least Cleo would not have to fear passing in front of André's big dogs. She had never seen a dog before, and I'm sure she would have been very frightened had the fence been erected in front of our apartment.

By the excited activity in the house, we gathered that André and his "new flame" were coming to visit. I decided to keep my cool and act as if nothing had happened. André-with the intervening of Simon who knew the local bank manager-had been able to arrange a showing of his and other artists' works at the bank. We attended out of curiosity, so I saw "Katja," André's new lover, for the first time. I tried to be polite and not let my prejudice influence my assessment of her. Very attractive in a cold calculating sort of a way, I thought. Time would tell if my impression was right!

I was surprised to see how Carla had changed! Katja had completely won her over, so it seemed. Although I had tried to hide my disapproval, Katja must have sensed it and probably knew that I wasn't fooled by her!

Sigrid and a friend were going away on a "health trip" to a resort, so she had stacked the freezer with food for the dogs that Katja came to pick up from time to time.

Every time she came, either Carla or she left the gate of the fence open with the result that the dogs would roam in the whole garden. So why had a fence been erected at all??

Fortunately I had been able once before to pick up Cleo and bring her to safety in the apartment. But would I always be so lucky? So I wrote a little note to Simon asking "would he please let me know before the dogs were coming so I could keep Cleo inside!" To my surprise, I found a note from Katja pinned on my kitchen door saying

"If I had a problem, I should see her personally because I was a bit too old to play games!"

My note had been addressed to Simon, so Carla and Katja had found my note and opened it! I was fuming! Simon, whom I confronted, was also appalled but he had no stand against the majority in this house.

When Katja showed up next time, I caught up with her and it was very unpleasant; she showed her true nature. She even attacked me by pushing me and using vulgar language, which only proved that my assessment of her had been right! But, upset as I was, I realized that something would have to be done!

Chapter LIII

Mario and I talked it over and-sad as we both were-we realized we could no longer stay in our apartment we both loved. So I offered Carla and Sigrid the option to buy my part of our inheritance. Their offer was too small to even consider. All of a sudden one of Katja's hurtful remarks came back to my mind! She had flippantly uttered "You are sick, and you will be out of your apartment and I will be in!" Was it possible that my apartment had been promised to André and Katja in expectation of my possible demise??? It was too horrible to even think that anyone of my family could be so low! But Katja's remark certainly left a cloud of suspicion on my mind. The atmosphere in the house was poisonous with everybody avoiding us. I had never experienced a situation to be so alienated from people I once loved. I badly needed some legal advice but could not afford to see a lawyer. An old school friend who was a retired judge told me of a place in Vienna City where some lawyers were giving free advice on a certain day. I was eager to take this opportunity.

When I arrived in the City Center, the streets were abuzz with people rushing around like ants chasing after something imaginary only important to them. I needed to calm myself and collect my thoughts into an orderly fashion so I could tell a lawyer of my dilemma. Our famous St. Stephan's Church in the City Center seemed to be the right place to find solace for my troubled mind. The cool and stillness in the church with the perfume of the flickering candles embraced me as if I had entered another planet. I found a bench in front of a corner altar hidden away from the main church center and the other visitors. Gazing into the Saint's eyes, I prayed that I would find a kind and understanding lawyer who would advise me how I could find a solution to my problems. I would have liked to stay longer, but I was on a mission that couldn't wait! I left the church much calmer than I had entered.

There were a lot of people and one had to wait until one's number was called. I was very nervous and tried to put order in my jumbled thoughts how I could best explain my situation to the lawyer. There seemed to be quite a number of them in attendance, and every time a door opened to see a client off after a consultation, I could also see the lawyer. Most of them were older; but I already had a favorite, a nice looking, and tall young man. How I prayed that my number would be called to see him! And, yes, my prayers were answered! I didn't know how to begin my sad tale; I was so nervous that I just burst into tears! After comforting me and listening to my story, he asked, "Had I ever thought of selling?" I replied, "Yes, but what my family had offered me was next to nothing. And apart from them, who would buy a third of a property that only consisted of two rooms and a bit of a corridor that had been converted into a bathroom and kitchen?" I had a photo of our villa with me, and when he saw it, he asked if I would consider selling to him if he and his Mother, after seeing it, were interested. So we arranged a meeting for the next weekend. The day came and his Mother was a lovely lady; we all soon were on first name terms. His name was Dieter and the Mother's name was Melody, a nickname that her Father had given her because she had a pretty voice and loved to sing. They liked what they saw and we soon came to an agreement. It was decided to keep the sale secret until the day of our departure.

Because nobody in the family wanted to talk to me, I didn't see any reason to inform them of my decision. It would be sad to leave the place where Mario and I had been so happy, but at least somebody would live there that I really liked. My heart ached when I thought that I would have to take Cleo away from her paradise where she spent the happiest 6 years of her life. Mario, who was back in the U.S. for a short visit, was amazed to hear my news when he called. How I longed to have him by my side right now!!

Chapter LIV

I was so happy when Mario had returned! Petra and only some close friends were told about our decision to permanently live in the U.S. They were not happy but understood our reason. Carla, who had never communicated much with Sigrid before, was spending a lot of time with her behind closed doors. I had a fair idea what they were talking about!

Our days were taken up by packing, flight arrangements, and hiring a shipping company who would pick up the big boxes with our belongings. Timing our departure and pickup of the boxes to coincide will be crucial!

We wanted to avoid another confrontation! André and Katja already tried hard to provoke that. I hardly dared to let Cleo outside anymore with "the lovers" positioned on a bench in front of our apartment and the two big dogs by their side. Mario found it hard to resist the temptation to stand up to them. But I convinced him by reminding him that he was an American and in a confrontation, they wouldn't hesitate to call the police and put the blame on him!

In our efforts to take care of all our arrangements, we must have had a lot of help from the "Great Beyond," because sometimes at the last minute, things went right that before looked like they were turning into a disaster. It seemed like I had been through all this turmoil sometime before!

On the day of our departure, we had smuggled Dieter and Melody inside early in the morning without anybody seeing them. The guys from the shipping company arrived to pick up the heavy boxes. "What have you got in them – bricks?", one guy exclaimed as they struggled to carry one out. With all the activity, Sigrid peered out from her kitchen and wanted to know "what was going on?" But she hurriedly closed the door when she saw me. I bet she got on the phone to André real fast, to tell him that it looked like we couldn't take the pressure anymore and that we were leaving. So now André and Katja could move into our now vacant apartment!!

Just as I was finalizing the paperwork with the pickup guys in the street, Simon came walking toward me, shook my hand and wished me "all the best." I did likewise; he apparently also thought we left the apartment in their favor! Petra and our friend had instructions to wait with the car on the other end of the street until the big van had left. Then they should quickly rush down to pick us up with our suitcases and drive us to the airport to catch our flight. Cleo wailed in protest which nearly brought the house down. It was heartbreaking!! Perhaps she remembered how this had happened once before when we left Australia! Just as we turned the corner in our street, Carla came "toddling" around with her shopping jeep. I don't think she even realized that we were in the car.

I only know the following happenings in the house from Melody. As soon as we had left, Dieter and Melody went to Sigrid's apartment to introduce themselves as the "new owners." After this shock, Sigrid cried in disbelief. "But this is my parent's home; you can't be the owner!!"

Carla, who had arrived just then, asked Sigrid innocently (like she probably did every morning while we still were there!), "Is there anything new??" (The "anything new" probably referred to Mario and me!)

When the realization of the truth sank in, I'm sure they all had a sleepless night trying to come to terms with the new situation. It was sad how a family relationship had ended because of greed by putting their own interests before the happiness of another family member! There was no hatred in my heart! What I did was my right and not meant to harm anybody. I hoped that eventually circumstances would work out for the benefit of everybody concerned!

Chapter LV

My second arrival in Philadelphia was not as pleasurable as the first. After Mario and I were separated because I had to go through the immigration procedures, a not so friendly security guard motioned me into a small room. Here I was, frightened and confused among other equally anxious people. What was the reason for keeping me from being reunited with Mario? I was sobbing quietly when Mario appeared. He was not supposed to be in the immigration area, but that hadn't deterred him. I was afraid that he was going to be "arrested" by a tough looking woman security guard. He reluctantly left reassuring me "not to worry," and saying in a loud voice that "he was going to call his lawyer."

A grumpy looking immigration officer waved for me to come to the desk and to be finger printed. I was so nervous that I didn't carry it out to the officer's satisfaction. He grunted at me: "Now you have spoiled it!" Some of my old fighting spirit returned, so I held up my index finger and growled at him: "I'm not a criminal so I'm not used to this! Here is my finger; do with it how you want it done!" After the finger prints were taken, I was ordered to sit down again. I was still wondering why--and how long--I was going to be detained when another security guard arrived and talked to the grumpy guy behind the desk, but left after a slightly heated discussion.

Minutes seemed to be like an eternity, but I was called to the desk again, my passport was stamped in a few places, and--still without any explanation--I was free to leave! There was a long flight of stairs down to the main hall. I was confused where to turn to find Mario and because I was still shaken by my experience, tears weren't far away.

I thought I recognized the security guard who had talked to "grumpy" upstairs before I was released. He was in a conversation with another security officer who had a beautiful German Shepherd dog on a leash. When they saw me unsure of where to go, they asked whether I needed help. They probably were touched when I sobbed like a little girl: "I have lost my husband and my cat!" The familiar security guard took me by the hand and said: "I'll take you to them" and the next minute I fell into Mario's worried arms.

Mario told me later that he was so upset after he saw me being held upstairs so this friendly officer had questioned him "what was the matter." When he heard Mario's complaint he offered to intervene and thus he became "my Savior" who speeded up my release.

He also told Mario that it was a well-known fact that some of the immigration personnel upstairs were not always very friendly. I confessed to Mario afterward that when I had been made so unwelcome by the authorities, if it hadn't been for him and Cleo, I would have gladly jumped on the next plane to get out of my predicament. Mario said he could hardly blame me for feeling that way! Mario's sister and husband, who were waiting outside to pick us up from the airport, must have been worried what had kept us so long. So the long drive to their house provided plenty of time to tell them the reason.

We were all glad when we arrived at their house. Poor Cleo was frightened and exhausted and went straight into hiding under our bed, where I had put water, food and her litter box. We were all ready for a badly needed good night's sleep!

Chapter LVI

Cleo had to be a house cat now. She wasn't very happy and probably still dreamed of the happy time in Austria. But she had our love and at least we were with her most of the time.

We hoped that we could save enough money for a down payment on our own house in the near future. However, that didn't happen for another two years. So we were glad that Mario's sister and husband rented two rooms to us.

We stayed in touch with Melody all the time, and we worried about her because she was experiencing the same hostile and nasty treatment by my sisters that we had to endure. All the rotten things they did to her made me feel ashamed that I once had loved them as part of my family.

Fortunately, Melody didn't have to live there all the time, but she could never be sure what they had planned to make her stay miserable!

I thought how stupid they were! In reality they were hurting themselves! What more could they wish for than to have a nice person live there occasionally who was taking care of a part of the property. But no, they extended their hatred for me onto Melody. One night when Mario and I were watching TV, I received a phone call from a friend in Australia. "Toni has passed away!" When I asked if it had been a heart attack, my friend replied: "No, he took his own life by shooting himself!" That was a shock, but it didn't cause me to cry. The love that once was there had been killed a long time ago.

Apparently with his alcohol addiction, he had lost his driver's license for the third time, which put an end to his driving days and he couldn't face up to that. Mario said I was lucky I had escaped from him in time.

Toni, in one of his rages, would have first shot Cleo and then me. I still don't know how I managed to get away! With Toni's suicide, another chapter was closed . . . We took stock of our savings and decided it was time to move on.

The house of our choice was in a nice area but property taxes were high. Nevertheless, we took on the gamble. We both liked the layout but hadn't realized how much needed to be restored and replaced. Every bit of money we saved went toward house improvements: replacement windows, a new roof, remodeling the 1-1/2 bathrooms and repainting nearly all the rooms took a lot of energy and money. Fortunately, Mario's cousin was a plumber and Mario was a "jack of all trades!" I helped where I could and promoted myself to be the "artistic director!" The garden was also my responsibility where I planted trees along the back fence line to provide privacy. Naturally, the trees attracted many birds that I started to feed. I overheard Mario one day saying to a visitor: "I'm glad that there are no elephants in this area because she would feed them too!"

So we never suffered from boredom and the years just flew past . . . .

Chapter LVII

Not long after the disturbing news from Australia, I received another call, this time from Austria. It was from Petra: "Carla has passed away!" Yes, I was sad, but it wasn't the Carla I once loved so I didn't cry.

Now, Dieter would have the opportunity to contact Karl to offer his sympathy for his Mother's loss, and at the same time to mention his interest to acquire Karl's part of the property! And it worked! Karl had often said that he was not interested to live there, nor did he even want to spend any money on repairs in the apartment. His Mother had to always take care of that. Sigrid and Simon had left for their yearly vacation after Carla's funeral. So now Dieter and Melody were in the majority after the deal with Karl was closed. They could now start the badly needed renovations and Sigrid and Simon would be forced to contribute to that.

When Sigrid returned, she rushed upstairs to see which of Carla's possessions were valuable enough to be of interest. But Melody had already changed the lock!! Naturally--in shock--she called Karl at his law office to find out the reason for the lock change. Karl, like the coward he was, had instructed his secretary to tell Sigrid that he couldn't refuse the wonderful offer to sell the apartment and wait until her return. The shock must have nearly killed her. Her own nephew had betrayed her!!!

Now they faced another hurdle, when they realized they needed to contribute toward Melody's renovation plans. Although Simon had a fabulous pension, most of it went to pay for André's debts and to maintain his extravagant lifestyle. I was curious how Sigrid was going to meet the challenge! But I would have to be patient until getting more news from Melody!

Chapter LVIII

I knew Sigrid well enough to not expect her to accept her latest defeat laying down. So I was not surprised when Melody reported to me that their peaceful existence was again threatened by another of Sigrid's schemes. They had bribed one of André's friends to impersonate a prospective buyer for Sigrid's apartment. This friend let it be known he planned to set up a music school after he was the new owner. They knew the noise with the loudspeaker blaring, plus the kids running around in the front garden, would drive Melody and Dieter crazy. To scare our friends even more, they set up the rumor that the apartment had already been sold to André's friend. My admiration for Melody will never cease! She bravely took it upon herself to drive to André in his "castle" and make him an offer. Of course, as we found out later, the whole setup was a scam to get as much money as possible!

After much haggling, greedy André accepted Melody's offer, and now my friends owned the whole villa! Sigrid and Simon moved into a rented house in a remote area near André. Eventually our friends turned the long neglected property into a show place, and I am sure my parents watched their efforts approvingly looking down from "Beyond." I was so happy that the place where I grew up was now in the hands of people who loved it and took good care of it!

Happy as I was, I became very concerned that Cleo's health was failing. She had been my faithful friend for 19 years and shared all my ups and downs in life. She suffered from the dreaded kidney disease and though we gave her dialysis three times a week, it didn't improve her condition. We spent the last night loving each other, and I knew I would have to make the decision that all pet owners dread having to make one day. But I knew in my heart she was going to a happy place called "The Rainbow Bridge." It is the place between heaven and earth where our pets wait for us when our time comes to leave. I missed her terribly but was grateful I could relive all the happy memories through the many photos of her. Now that our house had been made into a comfortable home, we felt confident that we could provide an invitation to Melody and Dieter to visit us. They accepted and spent a few enjoyable weeks in our company. Unfortunately, Mario had started to have a problem with COPD, which made it at times hard for him to breathe. So our house was only "headquarters" for our friends from where they could take tours or visit many museums. Mario's condition prevented us from accompanying them.

Happy times always go by too fast, so our friends left us but not before inviting us to spend time with them in Austria the next summer. The prospect of seeing them again so soon helped us to overcome the sadness of their departure . . . .

Chapter LIX

W e did take up our friends' invitation next summer! It was a wonderful feeling to be able to walk on the familiar grounds, and to see what a miracle Melody and Dieter had performed by bringing out the property's best features. All the years of neglect had been eliminated, and the garden was a park-like dream with an abundance of roses everywhere. Even the goldfish in the pond seemed to wear a "smile" with the fountain splashing cooling drops of water over the flowers nearby.

The three weeks were hardly long enough, especially when our other friends lined up as well to spend time with us.

Unfortunately, I could see that Mario's COPD was getting worse. When it was time to leave, I wondered in my heart had this been the last time to see all our friends?! After our return, I straight away made an appointment for Mario to see his lung specialist. He didn't seem to be very concerned but ordered for Mario to be on oxygen to be used when needed. We took up our usual lifestyle, and I thought how quickly the years speed past when one is happy!

Mario and I had been together for 18 years, and in all this time our Love had grown deeper! Life had been good to us, and we never regretted our decision to leave our troubles behind in Austria.

I even had my heart problems treated and never suffered another attack. When giving our marriage vows "for better or worse," most of us think that "the worse" would never come. When it does arrive, it gives us a feeling of helplessness and we begrudge it until we pull ourselves together and find a way to cope. That's how it affected me when Mario's COPD seemed to get worse and worse. So during our next visit to the lung specialist, I insisted for Mario to have a chest X-ray. When the report came back, it showed a devastating tumor, already too big to be operable. Yes, Mario received various treatments, but it was a long battle to no avail. Mario was a brave soldier who accepted his fate without complaining.

I don't know how I could have lived through all the worries and stress without the support of my faithful friends! Trish, a lady who lived further down on our street, was like my "Rock of Gibraltar." Because I had let my Australian driver's license run out, I depended on her to drive Mario and me to doctors' appointments, hospitals, and even to take me shopping. Many a time, she lifted my spirits because she knew from her own experience with her father's similar sickness what a tough battle I was facing. Joanne also was a great comfort to Mario and me, and each of her visits seemed to make our outlook a little brighter. I often thought of my marriage vows "for better or worse," but how much worse could it get?!

I finally had to ask help from "Hospice," and I was grateful I could be Mario's caregiver at home. Mario's concern was only for me and never was there a braver and more grateful patient in the whole world! I was so glad that Joanne insisted on staying with me that night when Mario departed to a happy place where one day we all will be reunited again! . . .

Chapter LX

Now that I am in the "autumn" of my life, I look back and can truly say that I have never been bored. Although I have experienced many "ups and downs," I am grateful for all of it. I regard the challenges as having been the testing ground for better things to come. I have found "true Love" with Mario, and I now have a new family. Joanne, with Louis' and Fran's approval from beyond, is like a "daughter," and Trish is like a caring "sister "that my own sisters never were!

So, I am not really lonely! I miss Mario, but I take solace in knowing that parting is necessary for the joy to meet again! I feel Mario's presence and I know when the time comes for me to join him, he'll be waiting . . .

Epilogue

Having listened to Melanie's story all these months, I became so engrossed that I sometimes felt it was "my life" I was writing about.

I rejoice in the fact that-according to Melanie-"True Love" really exists, and that the other uglier "Faces of Love" have no hope of tarnishing or destroying it.

It warms my heart when I see older couples still walking together holding hands! This provides me with hope that Melanie or I one day might do the same.

This will then be a glorious moment to be reunited with the "True Love" that only lucky people find after all the disappointments and struggles life can bring....